FID

06-12   7/13

2 6 JUL 2012   DOVER MOBILE

− 1 AUG 2013   STM
                                     3/18
2 3 AUG 2013   NLG
                                      5/19
− 6 SEP 2013
2 1 OCT 2013
1 4 MAR 2014
− 9 MAY 2014 1 8 DEC 2014
− 3 JUN 2015

2 4 JUL 2015
27/8/19

Please return on or before the latest date above.
You can renew online at *www.kent.gov.uk/libs*
or by telephone 08458 247 200

CUSTOMER SERVICE EXCELLENCE

Libraries & Archives

Kent
County
Council

00884\DTP\RN\07.07   LIB 7

D1147249

SPECIAL MESSAGE TO READERS

This book is published under the auspices of

THE ULVERSCROFT FOUNDATION

(registered charity No. 264873 UK)

Established in 1972 to provide funds for research, diagnosis and treatment of eye diseases. Examples of contributions made are: —

A Children's Assessment Unit at Moorfield's Hospital, London.

•

Twin operating theatres at the Western Ophthalmic Hospital, London.

•

A Chair of Ophthalmology at the Royal Australian College of Ophthalmologists.

•

The Ulverscroft Children's Eye Unit at the Great Ormond Street Hospital For Sick Children, London.

You can help further the work of the Foundation by making a donation or leaving a legacy. Every contribution, no matter how small, is received with gratitude. Please write for details to:

**THE ULVERSCROFT FOUNDATION,
The Green, Bradgate Road, Anstey,
Leicester LE7 7FU, England.
Telephone: (0116) 236 4325**

In Australia write to:
**THE ULVERSCROFT FOUNDATION,
c/o The Royal Australian and New Zealand
College of Ophthalmologists,
94-98 Chalmers Street, Surry Hills,
N.S.W. 2010, Australia**

DEATH AT DUNCAN HOUSE

Slim Harbin's last action on earth was to try and steal the car belonging to inventor Ramsay Duncan. As soon as he pressed the self-starter, the car and its would-be thief were blown asunder by a tremendous explosion. Death had come to Duncan House — and it was destined to come again, unless Detective Inspector Ian Boyd from Scotland Yard could prevent it. And if Boyd failed in his mission, the safety of the entire country was at risk . . .

NORMAN LAZENBY

DEATH AT DUNCAN HOUSE

Complete and Unabridged

LINFORD
Leicester

First published in Great Britain

First Linford Edition
published 2012

KENT
ARTS & LIBRARIES

Copyright © 1949 by Norman Lazenby
Copyright © 2011 by Brenda Birnett
All rights reserved

British Library CIP Data

Lazenby, Norman A. (Norman Austin)
Death at Duncan House. - -
(Linford mystery library)
1. Detective and mystery stories.
2. Large type books.
I. Title II. Series
813.5'4–dc23

ISBN 978–1–4448–1042–4

Published by
F. A. Thorpe (Publishing)
Anstey, Leicestershire

Set by Words & Graphics Ltd.
Anstey, Leicestershire
Printed and bound in Great Britain by
T. J. International Ltd., Padstow, Cornwall

This book is printed on acid-free paper

1

Night at Duncan House

Slim Harbin experienced a sudden thrill of fear when he reached the windowsill of the third floor room and looked into the face of a large, grim young man. Slim's expert grip on the drainpipe did not slacken however — there was some thirty-five feet between him and the ground — but his heart leaped painfully.

He had been told that Robert Duncan's house was likely to be unoccupied except for a skeleton staff of three servants who lived in the basement. This Larry Van Grote had told him — among other things. True to form, Larry had been playfully menacing. 'Slim,' he had said, 'I want a good job doing, and no mistakes. Get the stuff and deliver it to me personally, safe, sound, and all neatly tied up. Otherwise I shall be awfully mad at you, Slim — I shall be no end mad.'

And Slim Harbin, listening, had gently perspired. Slim had once seen the remnants of two of those who had incurred Van Grote's anger. It had not been a pretty sight.

Slim was no gangster. He might perhaps have been called a specialist in cat-burglary. Slim had entered some twenty-seven country houses in the British Isles, besides ultimately, a large stone house on Dartmoor, where he had subsisted for eighteen months at the Government's expense.

It was an unnerving moment for Slim Harbin.

'Come right in!' invited the young man pleasantly, and to ensure Slim's submission, he gripped the burglar's arm with steely fingers. Slim knew at once that he had missed his chance of a rapid descent. The young man's grip was like a vice, and Slim was badly placed to start struggling. Helpfully, the young man hauled Slim into the dark room.

'You know, you might have broken your neck,' said the young man reprovingly. 'Or I might have broken it for you. Now tell me your story. What are you after?'

'Who the hell are you?' gasped Slim, and he tried to wrench away his arm.

'Naughty, naughty!' said his captor, and easily tightened his grip so that the tears sprang to Slim's eyes.

It was a giant of a man who looked disgustedly down at Slim's bald spot, and Harbin stood five-foot eleven in his socks. But whereas Slim was inclined to weediness, the other man was magnificently proportioned. Slim realised that his chances of escape were small, especially when another attempt to free his arm resulted in that limb being twisted agonisingly behind his back.

'Let's get acquainted,' said the young man. 'My name is Ian Boyd, and you're a cat-burglar. I must say I admire the way you climbed that pipe. Didn't think I'd be waiting for you, did you? What are you after? Ramsay Duncan's safe? If so, you're on the wrong floor. The library is on the ground floor, old boy.'

He indicated a chair.

'Sit down.'

The tall man released Slim, who

collapsed dejectedly into the chair, and sat down on the corner of the bed, withdrawing from his pocket as he did so a heavy automatic pistol. He snapped back the safety-catch with a practised thumb. Slim eyed the weapon fearfully. He religiously avoided firearms — familiarity with which was too apt to breed a contempt that frequently led to the gallows.

Suddenly the moon broke away from the hurrying clouds, and a wan light invaded the room. Slim saw that his opponent possessed a pleasantly rugged face. Not exactly a film star sort of face, Slim decided, but still good enough for the dames.

'You know this is Ramsay Duncan's house?' asked Ian Boyd.

'Yeah.'

'Also that the family is away, and that only three servants live here?'

'Yeah. And who are you?'

'I've told you my name. Suppose you give me yours? And tell me what you're after?'

'So that's it!' Slim Harbin eyed the

4

other cautiously, then his long face loosened into a grin. From this moment he had a hunch he'd escape from this jam without feeling the heavy hand of the law on his shoulder.

'My name is Slim Harbin, pal,' he said thoughtfully, then: 'Mind if I smoke? And — mind telling me exactly what you're here after?'

'Smoke your head off if you like,' said the big man.

He fixed Slim with a pleasant but unswerving eye, and his strong hands grasped the end-post of the bed purposefully.

'Now — Slim — just why did you enter this particular room?'

'What the blazes d'you care? You don't belong to this joint!' rejoined Slim sulkily.

'Quite true,' drawled the other, 'I'm an interloper, like yourself. But you forget one thing, I've got a gun trained on you, and it's fitted with the latest device in silencers. How would you like me to blow a neat little hole through your head? Or rap your shins with the butt, like this?'

Ian Boyd made a sudden movement

with the pistol, his arm swinging in a long, swift arc. Harbin involuntarily jerked his legs clear, but the blow had not been meant to tell.

'Now spill it!' commanded Ian Boyd crisply, 'before I break your leg. Why this room?'

Slim said quickly: 'I got my orders!' He eyed the heavy gun with urgent distaste.

'Then you're not working for yourself? Who are you working for?'

Slim's lank jowls worked painfully, but he did not speak.

'Come on, friend — talk!' said the big man.

'I daren't tell you!' said Slim hoarsely.

Suddenly the gun thudded against his leg, striking perhaps three inches below the kneecap. Slim grunted with pain. He let his cigarette fall, and rubbed his leg vigorously. Ian Boyd carefully picked up the half-smoked weed from the floor, crushed it out with his fingers, and placed it in his pocket.

'You are a careless old cat-burglar,' he said, 'Now, have I to beat you over the head, or will you tell me who employed you for this job?'

Slim Harbin ceased nursing his leg just long enough to say: 'Larry did.'

'Larry who?' queried the other.

'Larry Van Grote.' Slim spoke carefully, as though afraid the owner of the name might suddenly appear through the floor to confront his hireling. 'But I'm not one of his regular boys — catch me working full-time for that swine! He promised me a hundred quid for this'

'Quite a lot of cash, Mr. Harbin.' Ian's face became curiously tense, and he leaned slightly forward. 'Now what've you got to lift for all that? The Crown jewels?'

Slim swallowed hard. 'My Gawd!' he said, 'I wish to hell I'd never taken this job!' He cursed profanely then said: 'Damn Van Grote and his blasted drawings! All planned, he said! Can't possibly slip up! Money for nothing — he said! Damn him!'

'So that's it!' said the big man, softly. He rose to his great height and looked down at Slim. 'Now,' he went on amiably, 'I can lay you out and then throw you from this window into the garden below

— you'd break your neck and they'd bring in a verdict of 'Accidental Death' which will be highly satisfactory — to me, if not to you — or,' he paused suggestively, and motioned with his gun towards the pallid outlines of a tall marble fireplace which shone dimly in the gloom, ' — or you can blow the safe, as I am sure you intended to do, and hand over the contents to me.'

Harbin's eyes glittered with professional curiosity.

'It's in the fireplace, isn't it?' asked Ian.

'Yeah. They sure choose some odd spots.'

Boyd nodded. 'They sure do!' He dropped his free hand into his pocket and produced a masked electric torch. 'Now, unless you want to make a sudden descent into the rosebushes, get to work!'

Harbin licked his lips. 'Larry'll kill me if I do this!'

'I'll kill you if you don't,' returned the other pleasantly. 'Now get on with it!'

Irresolutely, Harbin got to his feet and peered into the surrounding dimness. Ian Boyd switched on the torch, flickering its pale concentrated spotlight low around the room, focussing at last on the fireplace.

'Gawd!' breathed Slim, 'Aren't there some fal-lals!' He grimaced. 'Larry sure has all the dope. Told me the Duncan girl uses this room. A good-looking piece he said and the swanky heiress to a lot of dough.'

'I know all that,' said Ian, 'Let's get this safe open — I want those papers!' He thrust the gun against Slim's side. ' — *And* the package,' he added cheerfully. 'Come on — get out those expensive little tools of yours and set to work.'

They crossed to the fireplace which proved to be purely ornamental, for, falling to one knee, Boyd swiftly slid away an apparently solid section of the hearth-tiling to reveal a narrow steel plate set flush with the floor. There was a tiny control-knob for the tumblers, and a small aperture for a key. Slim knelt down and examined the safe appreciatively. Then he withdrew from his pocket a flat case and selected a feeler made of metal of paper thinness. A few moments' work convinced him that the safe was not fitted with burglar alarms. Slim brought out a tube of nitroglycerine-extract.

'I've a hunch you could open this tin can yourself, mister,' said Slim confidentially. 'I use 'soup' — like this!'

He shaped a little funnel from some soft wax and fixed it in the lock of the safe. Two more wax funnels were swiftly formed by Slim's deft fingers and placed flush against the faint line of the hinges. Into each funnel Slim then poured a minute quantity of his 'soup', and into each inserted a tiny detonator connected to a pocket battery.

'Get the mattress!' he said tensely.

They crossed to the bed, threw off the coverlets, and together carried the mattress across to the fireplace. They placed it over the hearth, and Harbin weighted it down with a selection of books and a solidly built tub-chair from nearby. All the time the blunt snout of Boyd's weapon followed his movements, but Harbin was too intent upon the task in hand to attempt to escape.

'Now,' he said in a low voice, and began to pay out the firing-wires towards the window. They paused for a second, silhouetted against the blue-grey sky, and Slim pressed the button.

A sudden, powerful thud came from the fireplace. The mattress billowed up and subsided.

'Good stuff!' said Slim professionally. 'They'll not hear that noise in the basement. Couldn't have found a better place for that tin can. That mattress muffled the row. Usually, this's where I grab the stuff, and beat it damned fast!'

'Not this time, Slim,' murmured Ian, rapping the pistol on the bedpost meaningfully.

Slim crossed to the fireplace. Without a word he pulled the mattress gingerly aside. The flashlight shone down. Harbin gave a grunt of satisfaction. He knelt and raised the door of the safe.

'Right-ho, Slim,' said Boyd calmly. He held out his hand. 'Give me those drawings, and that box.' Obediently Harbin handed out the contents of the safe — a slim sheaf of papers and a small, square box of cast-metal.

The memory of Larry Van Grote suddenly filled Slim Harbin with dismay. 'Gawd! I gotta get away before Larry knows I've messed the job up!' he said. Ian Boyd nodded. He replied gently: 'You needn't leave by the drainpipe, Slim. I'll show you down to the front door. That's the way I got in.'

★   ★   ★

Ten minutes later Slim was standing in the shelter of the thick privet bushes skirting the drive. He had left Ian Boyd in calm possession of the vaulted hallway of the Duncan House, utterly unperturbed.

Slim was full of mingled fear and annoyance. It had been an unprofitable night, for he would get no cash from Van Grote, and moreover he would live henceforth in fear and trembling lest he should again meet the gangster. Slim intended to leave for London as soon as he could reach a railway station, and with this idea in mind he turned his back on the silent house and set off down the path.

The night had grown chilly, and he turned up the collar of his short tight jacket, trembling momentarily with the cold.

Suddenly he stopped, listened, and with alacrity dodged into the cover of a rhododendron bush.

With a swift rush, a large car turned off the main road and whined into low gear as it began to climb the twisting gravelled drive.

Headlights swept the bushes in a remorseless tunnel of white light, which nearly caught Slim. He crouched, and remained bent double until the car stopped at the steps fronting the house's main entrance

Sudden curiosity caught at Slim Harbin. The Duncan House certainly seemed a busy little thoroughfare tonight! He paused irresolutely, blowing on his chilled fingers. Then, with an unexpected decisiveness, he made his way back towards the house, moving with a stealthy speed born of years of practice.

The low purr of the engine faltered, and was silent.

A man and a woman stepped from the car. The man had driven, and there was no other person left in the gleaming limousine as the two mounted the flight of wide steps leading to the hall door.

The watching Slim caught the glimmer of pearls about the girl's throat in the dimness, and the sheen of the man's shirtfront. The man produced a key and inserted it into the spring-lock of the door. As they entered the house, the girl laughed in a swift, unforced excess of gaiety.

'It's the Duncan girl and her father!' muttered Slim. 'Another bit of Larry's plan that's all screwy! Weren't supposed to be back before tomorrow!'

Slim's eyes glittered covetously. If he had a car like that, he could easily get to town without the necessity of buying a ticket to London or the risk of meeting some of Van Grote's numerous henchmen on the way.

But even as he watched the silent car, a tall figure strode swiftly from the shadow of an ornamental tree fronting the tall portico.

The new arrival was not identifiable to Slim — the car lights were extinguished, and the moon had passed behind a bank of cloud. But Slim gave a sarcastic grunt.

'Mr. Boyd, I'll bet! Guess the big lad has the same idea as me! He sure is a quick mover! Looks as though Duncan's going to lose his car!'

Ruefully Slim watched the tall, shadowy figure open the offside door of the car and enter. For a minute or two, the man sat as though working the controls, and Slim's eyes narrowed with surprise when the engine remained silent.

Suddenly the stranger ducked out of the car and melted back into the shadows of the tree.

Slim Harbin waited in breathless expectation.

Minutes ticked by. A dead, prolonged stillness possessed the night. Only a low rustle of moving leaves and branches disturbed the thick surrounding foliage. Apparently the tall man had gone his way.

'Changed his mind about pinching the drag,' said Slim. He looked nervously around. What was he waiting for? Wasn't this his chance to escape? Even if they heard the engine in the house, they'd be unable to stop him. Anyway, he could dump the car when he was well on the way to throw the cops off the scent, and perhaps hole-up for a while until things quieted down.

Slim darted forward and quickly reached the sleek machine.

As he climbed into the driver's seat, Slim grinned appreciatively.

'A posh drag,' he chuckled, and pressed the self-starter without wasting a second.

It was his last action on earth. With a stupendous thunderclap of sound, the car leapt asunder. Momentarily, a great rose of fire blossomed before the Duncan house, staining the night crimson with its ruddy glare. A faint echo of the explosion rolled among the distant hills even as the components of the shattered car crashed and whirled through the trees of the Duncan estate and clattered in ruin against the façade of the house.

Of Slim Harbin someone said later: 'You couldn't even tell it had been a man. There was just next to nothing left!'

2

Threat to the City

Larry Van Grote was of average height, but in compensation nature had endowed him with more than the usual width of shoulders. He was built like an athlete and at the moment his compact figure sported a suit that had cost some fifty guineas from a tailor of more than national reputation.

Larry was an exceedingly angry man on this particular morning, though — as was his habit — he restrained himself from lapsing into uncontrollable rage. When angry — as now — his blue eyes smouldered and his lithe movements became studiously slow — that was all. But those who knew him feared him most at such time. Larry Van Grote, in anger, had the fury and rapacity of an angry tiger.

'Last night's work was a washout, Nick,

he said slowly, 'Slim bungled the job and got his lot into the bargain. They've got what's left of him on two stretchers down at the mortuary.'

The man called Nick draped his long legs over the arm of an easy chair. He hoisted his knife-crease trousers an inch or so in a careful manner. His face was genial, and like his master he had startling blue eyes. He was about twenty-six years of age. His first conviction — at the age of nineteen — had been for robbery with violence: his successful use of a razor upon an elderly gentleman had somewhat prejudiced the jury against him, and Nick's customary haunts had missed him for five years.

He said confidingly: 'I'll get those drawings for you, Larry. But it'll have to be later, when the cops stop scrounging round the Duncan house.'

Van Grote did not reply at once. He put a lone cigarette holder to his lips and inserted a cigarette into it, with thoughtful care. He licked a gold lighter into flame and exhaled smoke fiercely.

'There's something I don't understand.

18

Who the hell blasted Duncan's car — and why?'

Nick shook his head. 'Don't ask me. Larry. I don't know. Somebody's got it in bad for Ramsay Duncan, I guess, that's all.'

'The papers are screaming their heads off,' said the other. 'Usual bilge about terrorism. You know the stuff: Bomb in Car at Duncan House. Unknown Man Killed! What are the Police Doing?' He grinned and thrust his hands into his pockets.

'The police — hell!' said Nick unpleasantly.

'Mind you, I wouldn't weep if Ramsay Duncan was blown to hell,' said Van Grote, 'once I've got those drawings.'

Nick shrugged.

'So we forget it, Larry,' he said easily, 'And when the bellowing's died down, I'll get those plans for you.' He eyed the older man speculatively. 'Is there much in it, Larry?' he asked.

A slow smile overspread Van Grote's aquiline features.

'There's millions in it!' he replied softly.

Nick watched his chief narrowly, as Van Grote went on:

'You know, Duncan might have had those drawings removed from that safe in the girl's bedroom. We've got to find that out. Perhaps the housemaid will talk again — if she knows anything, this time. She likes to step out for a gin-and-lime. I'll get Jim to pick her up again, and see if she can blow the gaff about that bedroom safe. As it is, I'm afraid Duncan might think somebody tried to blast him to get his drawings; and shift the damned things somewhere else.'

'It certainly looks like somebody is after those plans besides you, Larry,' said Nick, and Van Grote nodded slowly.

'Yeah,' he replied, 'After the drawings, Nick, and a little box — a beautiful little box.' He paused, then went on: 'At all events, I've got to get the stuff before — ' He broke off, and reached for another cigarette.

'Before — what?' prompted Nick.

'Before Ramsay Duncan destroys the lot,' came the unexpected reply.

'Will he destroy them, Larry?' Nick was

frankly puzzled. The prospect of any human being destroying a potential million pounds — or even a million pence — was outside Nick's range of comprehension.

'That's just what the old fool plans to do right now,' grunted Van Grote.

Nick debated whether he should ask for more precise information about the Duncan drawings — and the mysterious box — but Van Grote forestalled his question. He said: 'Now, Nick, don't make me mad by poking your nose into this too far. You know enough already. Perhaps too much . . . ' His voice became suddenly steely, and he eyed Nick with a cold speculation that made his henchman wince.

Van Grote continued: 'Anyway, there is somebody else after the stuff — that much I know. And that's all the more reason for Duncan deciding to destroy his handiwork pretty soon. He doesn't like the idea of his — um — workmanship becoming universally appreciated!' He laughed. 'Crazy old fool!' He stubbed out his cigarette viciously. 'But I need it, Nick

— and by God I'm going to get it!'

Van Grote suddenly rose, and motioning to the other to accompany him, walked across the luxurious apartment to where open french-windows disclosed a small balcony with a black-and-white tiled parapet. The two men emerged beneath a brilliant sky. From their vantage point they could survey the whole city, which lay spread beneath them, fading away finally into an uneven grey silhouette on the smoke-smudged horizon. The older man made a sweeping gesture.

'There she is, Nick,' he said tensely. 'No one-street town, either. With Duncan's little box — and with his drawings I could hold this whole city to ransom. I said there was millions in it, and I mean what I say. And there's a bigger city than this — called London! With Duncan's stuff there's no limit to what I could do even in London! I could create a situation in which the police wouldn't even dare to touch me! I'd take a rake-off from every fat pocket-book in the city. I could make the very Bank of England come through!

And I'd tell the cops to stay their distance. I'd be the Big Boss! They wouldn't dare to cross me, or else . . . '

'Or else . . . ?' asked Nick, curiously.

'That's just where you get too far ahead, Nick, at the moment,' said Van Grote with a chuckle. He turned on his heel and walked swiftly back into the apartment.

'Seems a big thing, Larry,' said Nick.

The other faced him with a little smile.

'You think I'm putting on an act, perhaps,' he said, gently, 'Maybe you think I can't put this over?'

'I think you can put it over, Larry,' replied Nick quickly. He smoked in silence for a while. Out of his depth as he felt, he did not mean his chief to observe his discomfiture.

'Fear!' chuckled Van Grote suddenly, 'That's the only weapon to use on these British and their thick-headed cops! Make them afraid to touch us and we can go the limit!'

'It's a good theory,' agreed Nick.

'Theory, nothing!' snapped Van Grote. 'Soon after I get that stuff of Duncan's into my hands, it will be an accomplished fact!'

He consulted his watch and sank into a chair.

'Now, Nick,' he said genially, 'Let's have a drink!'

In the afternoon, Van Grote had visitors. They came quite openly, knowing that if they were observed the police had no evidence of their many crimes to use against them. Van Grote had little need to hide his identity, for his own, malefactions were well concealed. He relied principally upon his wealth and his great native intelligence to exploit his many coups to the full — and on the fear of death to deter any would-be squealer.

The two men who stood before him were of vastly differing types.

'Take a seat, Jack,' said Van Grote, 'Cigarette, Ted?'

Jack the Gunner complied obediently, and sank into a hide-covered armchair with a single, neat movement. He was a thin-lipped, slight-waisted man with black, oiled hair. His suit was of a good, dark worsted, such as a professional man might wear. And, indeed, the Gunner resembled a lawyer, or perhaps a scientist, in the calm and dispassionate appreciation of his own particular profession — which was death.

Ted Morris merely smiled, and accepted the proffered cigarette.

If the Gunner had his place in the Van Grote mob as a deadly, efficient killer, Ted Morris, too, was a specialist in his own line.

Morris was a 'con' man — a wide boy, with a wide boy's gift of the gab, as the Gunner frequently put it. He never used a gun. Ted's tongue was his asset. He was a good mixer, too, surprisingly enough on speaking terms with many men of importance in the city, clubmen, men of business, and others. He was essential to Van Grote as an operative in affairs where violence was 'out'.

Ted was good-looking, blond, and easily moved to smile. He wore a well-tailored suit with nonchalance. Any business-executive looking for a well-bred junior would have approved Ted — as, indeed, several had from time to time to the general financial upset of their affairs.

'Good thing you're here, Ted,' said Van Grote. 'Still going the rounds with Duncan's daughter, I hope?'

Ted spread his carefully manicured hands and regarded them with satisfaction. He smiled.

'Of course, Larry. She likes me, and she's a decent kid.'

'Thinks he's the regular answer to a maiden's prayer,' interposed the Gunner, his lean face expressionless.

'Well, Shirley's a pretty thing,' commented Morris.

'And you belong to my mob,' said Van Grote calmly. 'So don't get any odd ideas about marriage, my boy. The girl's an heiress — and she might think you're amusing — but if you get serious about her you'll come up against the old man and he's a tartar. Besides, you take Shirley Duncan out on my money — and my time!'

Ted exhaled smoke elegantly, but his smile had become fixed.

'I want you to see her some more,' continued Van Grote thoughtfully, 'I want you to sound her about the bomb — ask her why anybody should want to blow up her father's car, you know the line to take. It's in all the papers, and your curiosity will seem natural. That explosion worries me — and I want every little bit of information you can get about it. Especially what the police think.'

'I'll see her tonight,' said Ted obediently.

Van Grote rose. He turned to the Gunner.

'And as for you, Gunner,' said Van Grote, 'I want you to stick around this place for a couple of days. Use the guest-room, and keep a rod handy. I've got an idea something might break.'

Jack the Gunner smiled and tightened his dark tie.

* * *

Ian Boyd turned into the lobby of his hotel and handed his coat over to the cloakroom attendant, receiving his ticket in silence.

He had booked his table earlier that

day, and was quietly escorted across the restaurant to a small alcove. He ordered dinner and a bottle of wine. When the waiter had gone, he looked incuriously about him.

A small orchestra was playing some popular melody but few couples were dancing. It was as yet early evening.

The headwaiter approached, and Ian Boyd gave short shrift to the excellent meal that was now placed before him. Food and service alike were impeccable. Boyd's view of the restaurant was a commanding one, and as he ate he watched all new arrivals with interest, but, when Shirley Duncan entered Ian frankly stared. She was escorted by Ted Morris. Ian knew much about this smiling girl with the lovely smooth features and gleaming brown hair, though they had never met. He also knew a great deal about Ted Morris, and his lips tightened ominously.

The couple sat down at a nearby table and began to talk animatedly. Ian watched them for some minutes, as discreetly as he could, though he found it hard not to stare at the almost perfect beauty of Shirley Duncan. Covertly he noted the gay curls of her chestnut hair, the courageous tilt of her finely-moulded chin, her ecstatic youth and vitality.

On a sudden impulse, Ian Boyd rose lazily and crossed to their table. Ian had just decided that he was much averse to the idea of Shirley Duncan enjoying Ted Morris's company.

'Good evening, Miss Duncan!'

She was momentarily taken aback. She looked inquiringly up at the tall man in evening dress whom she knew to be a stranger to her. Then, as his eyes unflinchingly met and held hers, her glance suddenly wavered, and she looked aside in some embarrassment.

Watching her, Morris guessed that the intruder was unknown to his companion. He nodded coldly to the big man, and cautiously awaited the next development as Boyd drew up a disengaged chair and sat down.

Ian was at his most genial, his most expansive. Ted Morris made as if to speak, but Boyd asked him placidly, 'And just what is the racket now, Tiresome Teddy?'

There was a silence. Ted Morris swallowed hard. He hated this stranger's air of command, his grim smile and above all else his large and capable-looking fists now suggestively adorning the tabletop. Ted experienced a sinking sensation in the pit of his stomach. Like all men of his kidney, Morris was physically a coward.

'This fellow is mad!' he blurted. He turned angrily in his seat as if to beckon a waiter. 'I'll have him thrown out!'

'Better not, Ted,' returned Ian. 'I'll lay ten-to-one you're on the Van Grote payroll — and Larry hates his boys to figure in common brawls — especially when they're likely to get damaged.'

Ted turned quickly round to the table again and moistened his lips.

'That's more sociable,' said Boyd. 'Are you giving London a miss nowadays, Teddy? We were just becoming interested in you, old boy.'

Shirley Duncan regarded the two men calmly. But when she spoke, she addressed herself to Ian.

'Would you please admit me to this little tête-à-tête?' she asked. 'And will you please explain who you are?'

Amusement gleamed in Ian's eyes.

'I, Miss Duncan, am a man who intends to become a friend of your father — a close friend, I trust. In point of fact, I shall call upon him tomorrow and thereafter stick like a leech.' He grinned. 'My name is Ian Boyd and I am a Detective-Inspector from Scotland Yard.'

3

Inspector Boyd Explains

A short silence followed Ian's words, then: 'Does my father expect to see you?' asked Shirley quietly.

'No. It is just a friendly visit,' said Ian. She said 'Oh!' then she was silent again.

Ted Morris tried to repair matters as best he could. 'Possibly you're looking into this extraordinary business of the explosion?' he queried. Inwardly he was cursing, but he talked smoothly on. 'Shirley and I have discussed it. I can imagine this being a great shock to Mr. Duncan, to say nothing about the loss of a dashed good car. I . . . '

'It was a shock to me,' said Ian gravely, and his eyes gleamed with mischief. 'But it is just as great a shock to see Mr. Duncan's daughter dining with an accomplished crook. You were just a small-time hoodlum when I knew you in London, my lad, but now — hey presto! — now I find you in charming company in a most distinguished hotel. Reformed, Ted?'

The other swallowed.

'You're making a mistake . . . ' he began.

'No mistake, old boy, no mistake at all. And I hear that Larry Van Grote is the Big Boy in these parts. You work well for Larry, Ted, I should think. Oil and vinegar, as the proverb has it.'

'I don't know what you mean,' snapped Morris. Ian turned to the girl.

'That is treasonable,' he said sadly. 'What a blow to the boss's dignity! If only he could hear Tiresome Teddy now.'

'Don't call me that, damn you!' snarled the other.

Shirley Duncan was looking at Ted Morris with a startled expression.

'Surely this is not true, Ted?'

'An absolute rigmarole!' snapped her escort. 'Come along, Shirley. Let's get out of here. They seem to admit any riff-raff.'

But when they rose, Ian accompanied

them coolly to the foyer. Shirley Duncan eyed the big man covertly. She also glanced at Morris, but he looked most uncomely at that particular moment. Shirley therefore turned her attention back to Ian Boyd. *He*, certainly, was quite unperturbed.

Somewhat subdued and a good deal puzzled, she went for her cloak. When she returned to the lobby, she found the two men waiting for her. The big man was smiling, charmingly, but Ted Morris remained unimproved by a scowl, and had somehow grown suddenly ordinary.

And when she climbed into a taxi outside, both men entered and sat one on either side of her.

'Look here, have I to call the police?' demanded Ted Morris suddenly. He felt the situation was distinctly out of hand, and had decided to try to retire without losing face. Above all else he felt worried about Van Grote's reaction when he learned that a special investigator from Scotland Yard had appeared to warn Shirley Duncan that her friend was a crook.

'I am the police, old boy,' replied Ian mildly. 'And I intend to escort Miss Duncan home.'

Like a drowning man Ted Morris grasped at a straw. He felt pretty certain that his contact with the girl would not exist tomorrow, anyway.

'I'm sorry, Shirley,' he said coldly, 'But if this fellow intends to impose himself on you, I feel I'd better go.' He descended from the taxi with all the dignity he could muster, and Ian Boyd laughed aloud at his vanishing coat tails.

Then the big man rapped on the glass panel behind the driver's head. He said 'Duncan House, my friend.'

★ ★ ★

Ian Boyd leaned back against the cushions of the taxi.

'On second thoughts, I see no reason why I should wait until tomorrow to pay my visit to your father,' he said. 'He is at home tonight, you know.'

She did not ask how he knew this, but put another question to him.

35

'Are you serious in what you said about Ted being a crook?'

'Crooked as a dog's hind leg. I hope you won't pine for his company. I can't be sure he is working for Van Grote — though in the circumstances I'll soon find out — but if he is, I very much fancy that he would just adore — er — borrowing your father's drawings.' He watched her steadily as he spoke, and saw that his knowledge had alarmed her. But she quickly recovered her composure.

'What do you know about the plans?' she asked quietly.

'I know a little about them — that they compose one of the most dangerous documents in the country for one thing. I have learned also that Van Grote would like to obtain them, he does nothing without reason. Then there are others who are also interested. And *they* have *their* reasons! Therefore, the Home Office is anxious — as Home Offices always are — and have briefed the Commissioner of my Special Department, who in turn has passed the job on to me. That's the way of the world.'

Shirley said abruptly: 'Do you know that the drawings were stolen last night, and that, if they had not been taken, my father would have burned them by now?'

'Burn them, would he?' commented Ian. 'Well, that's in line with his attitude. Idealist, isn't he?'

The girl nodded.

'He may be an idealist, but he is not a fool,' she said warmly. 'I have some idea of the significance of his secret, but that is all. I agree with him that the drawings should be destroyed.'

Ian shook his head reluctantly, then he replied: 'Let us look at the facts of the case. For eleven years your father works in absolute privacy after retiring from a most brilliant scientific career. He issues no statements, he refuses to see the press. But, you know the most carefully kept secrets have a habit of leaking out. And so — ' He paused and thoughtfully regarded the swiftly passing pavements with their busy throngs — 'And so we *know* what I think you've *guessed*.'

'What is that?' she asked, guardedly.

'That your father has at last perfected a

new explosive of gigantic power,' he replied, and heard her gasp. He went on: 'An explosive substance of almost atomic destructiveness, but cheap in production, safe to handle, and able to be produced from easily obtained chemicals. In short — the technicians', the soldiers' — and the crooks' ideal explosive.'

'How do you know this?' she queried in a low voice.

The big man grinned.

'We know what we know,' he said, 'And we're also pretty certain that your father has prepared a quantity of the explosive — which we call by the code-name 'thuramite' — for experimental purposes. In fact,' he concluded easily, 'You have recently been sleeping next to a small metal box full of it, walled up in the hearth of your excellent bedroom, together with your father's formula and plans of the rather nifty little machine that must be used to detonate the stuff.'

She looked suddenly startled, but he waved a hand reassuringly.

'Don't bother,' he said, 'The stuff is quite safe. It can only be detonated by your father's machine — which is half the secret — or by the application of great heat. The machine exists only on paper — and your beautiful chimney-piece is a blank — just a false flue, as I ascertained.' He laughed joyously.

Her lips parted in amazement.

'So it was you — ?' she breathed.

He nodded.

'Yes, indeed. Or, rather an unfortunate devil named Slim Harbin.'

To his admiration and relief, she expressed no fear at his admission, but said, simply:

'Why did you want the plans of the detonator — and the formula?'

He gestured.

'Let's not discuss that for the moment. Just remember two things, please. One, your father's drawings repose at the moment in a belt strapped tightly about my own athletic and muscular waist; two, a couple of exceedingly dangerous characters, Larry Van Grote and Marcus Williams are after your father's secret. And they'll stop at nothing to get it. Not even at planting a bomb in his car to dispose of him so that these plans may become more vulnerable during the settlement of his estate, and so that he may — er — depart this life before destroying the permanent record of his discoveries.'

This time she was really afraid. Her face paled, and she placed her hand to her throat.

'Did Van Grote do that?' she whispered.

'No,' he replied. 'Williams. He is a bomb expert — he likes his victims to make a spectacular exit. He operated in the States for a time. An old trick of Marcus's that! A bomb fixed to the ignition system of the car. You start the motor and — goodnight!' He chuckled grimly. 'Yes,' he said meditatively, 'It has every hallmark of Williams's work. He must have been hiding in the grounds when your father drove up. He laid the trap for Mr. Duncan — but Slim Harbin sprang it!'

She looked at him. 'So the body — ?' she shivered, and left the question incomplete.

'Was Slim Harbin's.' He explained swiftly: 'Harbin was sent by Van Grote to blow your safe. I caught him at the house and made him finish his appointed task, taking from him the plans and the thuramite. Then I turned him loose. When you drove up, I made my exit through a back window.'

She was more composed now, and added thoughtfully: 'And this man — Slim — thought he'd steal daddy's car?'

'Yes. For his getaway. Poor devil! He got away all right!'

She remained solemn-faced in spite of his grim humour. Then she said: 'It wasn't a pretty sight. You see I found him — what was left.'

'I'm sorry,' he said gently, and she smiled.

'It's all right,' she said, 'I'm pretty well self-possessed, when the occasion demands.' She paused. 'But these men — Van Grote and Williams — why are they so interested in daddy's work?'

He lit a cigarette with thoughtful care.

'Well,' he replied at length, 'Suppose the Prime Minister one day receives the

41

pleasant information that hidden somewhere in — say — London, there is a
parcel, little bigger than a suit case, which
upon exploding will create almost as
much havoc as an atom-bomb. Supposing
this information were coupled with an
unconditional demand for a million
pounds in gold, to be delivered from
government stocks, or else — ' He
grinned mirthlessly.

'Or else the thuramite explodes?' she
questioned calmly.

He nodded. 'You've got it. You see, we
can't detect the stuff by its radiation
— which the boys might do with an atom
bomb — and its very smallness removes
the necessity for special precautions in
assembling and concealing the finished
bomb.' He shrugged. 'The possibilities of
blackmail on a national scale are infinite
— and appalling.' He drew strongly on
his cigarette and exhaled luxuriously.
'Add to all this,' he continued, 'the fact
that a good chemist, equipped with more
or less normal laboratory equipment
could manufacture the explosive fairly
easily, and safely, and you know,' he

concluded softly, 'why the authorities are windy — in a big way!'

'No wonder daddy intends to destroy his secret,' she said thoughtfully, and the big man spread his hands in a gesture of resignation.

'That's what I told 'em,' he replied. 'Let him put a match to the thing and good riddance! But the people in Whitehall won't have it that way. They want the formula of your father's explosive and the plans of his detonating machine for the armed forces.' He chuckled. 'And in the present state of international affairs, who can blame 'em?'

There was a silence. Shirley Duncan placed her hand to her lips, and puckered her brows in thought, then she said:

'Do these men work alone?'

'Williams and Van Grote?'

She looked at him and nodded.

'Van Grote runs what you'd call a 'gang'. Williams works mainly alone, sometimes abetted by a woman called Myra, who passes for his wife. As we see it at the moment, Larry is probably interested in the possibilities of putting the screws on H.M. Government by means of a threat to blast what the dailies call our 'throbbing metropolis'. Williams, on the other hand, is less ambitious — though just as poisonous — and is probably working for a foreign power. Neither of them will stop at anything.'

Shirley looked out of the taxi window and saw that the suburban bungalows were thinning out, giving way to roads lined by fields and hedges. Recognising various features of the landscape, she knew that they were not far from her home. Ian Boyd said: 'Anyway, I hope your father will see eye to eye with the authorities, and hand the plans over to them. Point of fact, whatever my own inclinations in the affair, I intend to do my level best to persuade him to just this course of action. Can I ask you to try your powers of persuasion upon him?'

'Perhaps,' she said enigmatically. 'In any case, the thing is too big for daddy. He is terribly concerned about the potentialities of his discovery. He hasn't even told me more than he released in a speech to a private gathering of scientists some weeks ago.'

Boyd smiled. 'It was that meeting which gave us our first definite information,' he said. 'They were sworn to secrecy — but somebody talked. Scared, I suppose, by the size of the thing. Then the Home Office acted — and here I am. In fact,' he added gently, 'Here we are!'

'Very much without Ted Morris,' she returned impishly, and laughed aloud.

His laughter joined hers. 'Ted's a wrong 'un,' he said. 'Not the ideal escort for a lady.' He spoke reflectively, 'One day I'll spoil that pretty face of his and put him permanently out of business.'

She regarded him mockingly. 'Do you infer, Mr. Boyd,' she asked, 'that I'm a fool for a pretty face?'

'Who knows?' he demanded, 'You should at least try a change once in a while. For instance, I'm no great beauty, but I have a heart of gold.'

She did not reply, but in the alternate light and shade of the cab, he saw her smile.

Suddenly the vehicle swung off the

main road into the driveway leading to Duncan House.

'Here we are,' she murmured. 'Daddy is at home.'

The car stopped, on her instruction, before the tall portico of the house, and they descended into the now moonlit dusk. The driver approached them, and Boyd drew out his wallet, extracting a crisp note.

There came a sudden snapping report from the shrubbery, a swift angry crack in the air as though a whip had been snapped.

The taximan gasped abruptly. His knees buckled. A sudden smear of blood appeared on his temple, spread, became a hideous red mask obscuring his pale face.

Even as the dead body hit the gravel of the pathway, Ian Boyd seized the girl and dragged her down to her knees. The next two shots whined above them, and Boyd heard the glass of the taxi's windows tinkle onto the running board.

4

Shirley in Danger

Hugging the ground, Boyd lay still. Cautiously, he raised his head and watched the black mass of bushes ahead, from which the shots had come. At the moment, the body of the luckless taximan afforded them some cover, but Boyd realised only too well that the assassin might approach them to finish his job at close quarters. The shrubbery remained silent, however.

Boyd gripped the shoulder of the girl at his side.

'When I give the word,' he whispered, 'follow me for all you're worth.'

She made no reply, but he felt her arm grow tense in his grasp. 'Now,' he said abruptly, and, rising, they ran at a crouch for the nearby grass verge. Still no more shots. All was silent. Panting, they burst into the bushes and undergrowth of the garden, Boyd drawing his automatic as he

47

ran and slipping off the safety catch.

Suddenly his companion caught his arm. They had struck a narrow pathway. 'The kitchen door!' said Shirley. Together they made for the house, found the door, only to feel it resist their pressure. Shirley Duncan beat on the panel with her clenched fist.

'Marion! Marion!' she called urgently.

The door suddenly opened, and a stout woman in a cook's apron confronted them, her mouth open in fear and surprise.

'Quick!' snapped Boyd. He thrust the startled domestic aside, pulled Shirley headlong into the room, and slammed the door, forcing home the heavy bolts.

'Where's Mr. Duncan?' he demanded.

'In the library, sir,' said the woman, 'What were those bangs?'

Boyd made no reply.

'We'd better get to your father, Miss Duncan,' he said, and Shirley nodded.

'Don't open the door to anybody, Marion,' she directed, then motioned Boyd to follow her.

The library opened off the hall, and its doors were open. Ramsay Duncan was standing calmly at the huge windows, gazing out into the grounds from the cover of the heavy curtains.

'Better keep away from the windows, sir,' Ian advised, and without a word the scientist simply stepped back and pulling on the long cord swept the curtains across the twilit expanse of glass. Then he turned and stood impassively regarding his daughter and her escort. 'Cool devil!' murmured Boyd.

The owner of Duncan House had been aware enough of his danger to switch off the lights before moving to his vantage point. Now he pressed the switch of a standard lamp, just visible in the flickering fire-glow, and a sudden radiance illuminated the room.

'Are you quite all right, Shirley?' he demanded, and crossed to the girl. He kissed his daughter calmly and formally, as though greeting her in circumstances far removed from the present strange drama. Then he turned to Boyd.

'And who are you, young man?'

'I am Detective-Inspector Boyd, of the special branch of Scotland Yard,' replied

Ian. In the face of this composed and dignified man, he felt oddly embarrassed — rather like a small boy surprised by his headmaster, eating in class. He thumbed on its safety catch and dropped his automatic back into his pocket.

'One moment,' said Duncan, almost apologetically.

He crossed the library softly, closed the heavy doors, and slid fine steel bolts into their sockets.

'The hall door is quite firmly secured,' he said as he returned, 'My dogs became restless about a quarter of an hour ago, and I thought that my estate had perhaps been — er — invaded again.' He paused. 'And then, when I tried to telephone the police and found the telephone dead, I guessed that I was likely to be — er — attacked. Two minutes later your car arrived and was fired on. I must thank you for my daughter's safety . . . ' He withdrew a handkerchief, and dabbed at his lips, and looking closely at him Ian Boyd could see the fine beads of sweat on his face and brow. Even Ramsay Duncan's iron reserve could not stop nature betraying his anxiety for the girl he loved more than his very life.

'I thought there were police guards here?' said Boyd.

'There were,' replied the older man, 'But I used my influence with the authorities to have them removed. I do not like to have my private life watched too closely — not even by policemen, Mr. Boyd,' he concluded quizzically.

He shrugged. 'Not a pleasant life for a quiet scientist — first my motor car blown up, together with a strange gentleman who was apparently attempting to — er — borrow it, then large numbers of policemen crawling about my grounds, and now . . . '

Boyd broke in evenly: 'A dead man in your front drive, and gunmen on the point of paying us a visit as likely as not.'

Duncan's eyebrows rose. 'A dead man?'

'The taximan. Shot through the head,' Boyd said, 'It might have been wiser to have kept a few clumsy policemen handy, Mr. Duncan.'

Duncan's face clouded, then he said 'I'm sorry.'

Boyd pursed his lips. 'One thing you might like to know, Mr. Duncan: your plans are safe, so is the thuramite.'

Duncan looked up swiftly, his brows contracting.

'Oh, and how d'you know?'

'Because, at the moment, your papers are residing on my person, and the thuramite is locked in the safe of the Chief Constable of Bannockfield . . . '

'I see,' said Duncan icily, 'You . . . stole them.'

Boyd nodded. 'Call it that if you wish. At all events, I acted in the capacity of an agent of the Home Office — whether legally or illegally.'

'Illegally, I think,' returned Duncan. He extended his arm. 'Now if you will please return my property . . . '

Suddenly a dog barked somewhere outside, with a swift crescendo of throaty cries that echoed in the still hush of the night. Duncan spun on his heels to face the window.

'Our friends are still here,' he said softly. 'Quick!'

He flicked out the lamp, and crossing

to the heavy curtains, drew them aside. The pale light of a quarter-moon filtered into the room. The raucous barking of the watchdog continued steadily.

'Go to the other curtain,' Duncan called softly, and Boyd obeyed.

'You will find shutters behind the curtains which we can bar across the windows,' said the scientist. 'Now!'

As quickly and silently as possible, Boyd and Duncan, withdrew the heavy oak shutters which folded concertina-wise on each side into the thickness of the wall behind the drapery, and carefully closed them into position across the great windows, shutting out the moonlight and enshrouding the room in a velvety blackness lit only by the flickering of the dying fire.

With a sigh of relief Duncan dropped home the locking-bar.

As it clicked into place the shutters suddenly jerked with the full weight of a heavy blow. Splinters of wood spurted from the panels. There came the swift cascading of glass.

Instinctively the men crouched, and

Shirley dropped to her knees in the shelter of a heavy settee of crimson brocade, which occupied the middle of the floor.

'Get back!' commanded Boyd, and he and Duncan joined the girl at a stoop.

Duncan said reflectively: 'I think we can stand up here. There is a drop of about fifteen feet from the windows into the sunken garden, and unless they're shooting from some distance, the line of fire will take the shots well above our heads.'

They rose cautiously, and Shirley went carefully across to a small table by the wall, where she switched on a shaded reading-lamp, filling, the room with a pale rose-coloured light.

Without a word she pointed. High up on the wall a long mirror showed a shattered face, the bullet hole making a dark circle in the back-plate. 'I thought so,' said Duncan, 'They're firing at close range.' He turned to Boyd. 'You have a gun?'

Ian nodded, and produced his automatic.

'Ten shots,' he said, 'And our friends probably have a couple of tommy-guns — silenced, now, into the bargain.'

'Yes,' agreed Duncan, 'I certainly didn't hear the report of that last shot.' He looked at Shirley. 'I'm afraid we're in a rather difficult position, my dear,' he said gently.

The girl threw up her chin defiantly. 'They've got to get in at us first,' she stated calmly. 'And we have at least ten bullets.'

'Good girl!' said Boyd, and his eyes lit with admiration. 'They're probably afraid to tackle the house — that's our one strong point. They'll probably just hole up outside, and snipe at whatever they see for a while. So at least we've got a little time!'

Abruptly a tattoo of blows rained on the outside of the library door. The terrified voice of Marion, muffled but audible, supplemented the frantic knocking;

'Let me in! Let me in, Mr. Duncan!' she cried. 'Some men are smashing in the kitchen windows!'

Ian Boyd slipped the bolts, drew the terrified Marion into the room, and threw the doors to again, securing them as he did so.

'Quick,' he called to Duncan, 'Get this across the door!' He ran to a large sideboard, which flanked the doorway, and Duncan and he threw their combined weight against it. Luckily the sideboard was equipped with heavy ball castors and ran into position without undue effort. They pushed it hard up against the grained panels, and reinforced it with a heavy oak chest, which required all their strength to lift.

'Now,' commanded Ian, 'Stand along the wall and take whatever cover you can. You women go into the alcove there. Don't move forward whatever happens, for if they fire at an angle through the door they may hit you.'

Shirley half-pushed, half-pulled the almost fainting cook into their refuge, and the men took up their positions with their backs to the wall and as far from the door as possible.

They waited. Two, three minutes

passed, but all was silent. Then, suddenly, there came the sound of swift footsteps in the hall outside. The doors shook slightly as somebody tried them, then more violently as a shoulder was applied. A voice spoke urgently, then came a shout: 'Open up in there if you want to stay healthy!' In spite of the closed and barricaded doors, the voice was reasonably distinct. Ian turned towards the others, and placed his finger to his lips. Still they waited, in silence.

There was a pause, then their attacker shouted:

'We know you're in there. We mean to have the plans — or Duncan! Take your choice. We've a man watching the window, if you drop the papers out within three minutes we'll clear out — or, if you like, the old man can volunteer to accompany us for a little chat. D'you hear, Boyd?'

Ian grinned. Ted Morris had been quick in contacting his confederates, or perhaps a London member of the gang might have recognised Ian.

At all events, the fight was well and truly on.

'Nothing like firing the first shot,' whispered Boyd to Duncan, 'Let's try their strength!'

The voice spoke again: 'Three minutes Boyd then we get tough!'

Ian stepped smartly forward, raised his arm, and fired a shot obliquely at the exposed upper panels of the door. Shirley screamed piercingly. There came a sudden rattle of footsteps in the hall as the gunmen scattered. Then, again, silence.

'Now for it!' murmured Ian.

They had not long to wait. The doors suddenly thundered to the impact of giant blows. Great splinters of wood tore and whirled into the room. Thrust open by the blows of the bullets, the sideboard doors burst grotesquely ajar, spilling cutlery, linen, and shattered bottles onto the parquet flooring. In the middle of the room, the settee teetered like a live thing, its upholstery leaping asunder as though ripped by great invisible claws.

For perhaps thirty seconds the fusillade continued then silence fell, abrupt and almost sinister by comparison with the late frantic kettledrumming of the shots in the room.

'Thought so,' breathed Boyd. 'Tommy-gun! Fifty-round magazine, and we got the full benefit!'

'Listen, Boyd,' came the voice through the shattered. door, 'we've got plenty more where those came from. And we've got grenades.' Boyd tensed, and his face set grimly. The speaker continued: 'So, unless you want us to blast you all, go to the window and drop down those plans. If you haven't got the plans, we'll take Duncan — the hard way.' There was a silence. 'Well?'

Boyd turned to Duncan, his face expressionless.

'It's no good, sir,' he said, 'They've got us. I'm afraid it's the plans, or you, or the end for us all.' As he spoke, his voice gradually gathered in volume. Suddenly he turned his head again towards the doorway, and shouted: 'Okay! You win, damn you!' He placed his hand inside his coat and withdrew a sheaf of papers, bound tightly in oilskin. 'Here they come!' he cried.

'My plans!' gasped Ramsay Duncan, 'My formula!'

For once his cast-iron composure had fled. 'You cheating devil! I'll see us all dead before I'll let you hand those over!'

He seized Boyd by the throat. 'Give them to me! Give them to me, I say!'

The big man jerked his head free from the scientist's grip and struck upwards, once, with his clenched fist. Ramsay Duncan gave a choking sob and sank unconscious to his knees, Boyd grasping his coat-lapels to steady his descent.,

'Sorry, old fellow,' he murmured, 'But that's the way of it!'

In a second, Shirley Duncan was at her father's side, her eyes flaming with rage. 'How dare you strike my father!' she cried.

Boyd replied simply, urgently: 'Stay with him, Shirley, and trust me!'

Then with a swift easy stride he crossed to the windows, removed the locking-bar, and having eased open the shutters, tossed the package through into the darkness.

5

Kidnap — and Escape!

Marcus Williams and the woman who called herself Myra Williams waited patiently enough in the shrubberies of the Duncan House. Their long black roadster was parked on the main road, drawn well in beneath the hedgerow, its lights doused.

Myra said softly: 'They've gone in, now.'

Marcus nodded. 'Yes. They're Van Grote's men all right. They mean business, too. That taxi-driver I looked at is dead as mutton.' He lowered his voice apprehensively. 'The Gunner's with them! They burst in through the kitchen!'

Myra laughed softly, cynically. 'Scared of the Gunner ain't you, Marcus my lad?'

Williams replied: 'I like to stick to the tools of my trade — and they don't include razors and bullets.' He chuckled.

'I just like to see a nice big bang once in a while my dear.'

'You nearly saw one too many when you blew Duncan's car my boy, returned the woman, 'Our friend from the Continent was awful mad, Marcus. He made himself quite clear about us keeping Duncan very much alive. So take care, Marcus, no more brainwaves, no more short cuts.'

Williams shrugged, then asked: 'Did you see anything on the other side?'

'Yes. They've got a lookout under the big windows round the corner. I couldn't see much, but while I was round there, he took a shot at somebody. He was using a silencer, too.'

'I don't think they'll meet much opposition,' breathed Williams. 'There's only the cook in, and old Duncan's had the cops called off.'

'There's Boyd!' said Myra, and her voice was not pleasant.

'Yes,' agreed Williams, 'There's Boyd.'

Suddenly the woman said: 'Listen!'

They stood motionless, hardly breathing. From the direction of the house came a swift, regular crackling noise like the much-diminished sound of a child running a stick over iron railings.

'Tommy guns!' said Williams. 'Silenced, as well. They're shooting somebody up!'

The firing ceased as abruptly as it had begun, and for perhaps three minutes an eerie silence enveloped the estate. The man and woman did not speak, but concentrated all their attention on the house.

Suddenly the dim figure of a man ran down the front steps. A second figure detached itself from the shadows, and joined him. There was a brief consultation, and a flashlight shone out, illuminating what appeared to be a book, or map, which the second man was holding.

The flashlight snapped off. Shrilly, penetratingly, a whistle sounded.

More men emerged from the house, with purposeful speed. For a moment they gathered into a tight knot of figures, which then swiftly broke up, the gunmen making off down the drive in a sort of open order. Williams counted them silently as they passed down the moonlit drive and melted away into the shadows. There was a pause, then from the road came the swift snarl of powerful engines, which whined into a crescendo, and died away.

'Seven!' breathed Williams, 'That's all there were with the guy you saw!' He turned to Myra. 'Wonder what they left behind?'

'Let's go and see, Marcus,' said his partner sweetly, 'And don't get scared.'

He hesitated, then followed her cautiously. The thickly-scattered leaves of the shrubbery crackled beneath their feet.

They gained the drive, crossed it, and were approaching the house, when a man and a woman emerged from its open doors and ran down the steps.

Marcus Williams seized Myra by the shoulder and drew her swiftly into the cover of the stationary taxi, beside which lay the rigid body of the taxi-man, the head ringed by a dark sluggish halo.

Myra gasped urgently; 'It's Boyd and the Duncan girl!'

Shirley Duncan seized her companion

64

by the arm, and exerting her strength halted the big man and compelled him to turn to face her. She said: 'Why did you do it? Why? Daddy will go crazy when he knows!'

Boyd replied: 'Wait, Shirley, and trust me. Just let's satisfy ourselves by getting the police as soon as we can.'

The girl raised her hand to her mouth and for a second seemed about to surrender to tears. Then she said: 'All right. If you want it that way. We'll talk afterwards.'

The hidden watchers saw the couple turn to face in their direction. Williams whispered suddenly: 'Myra! This is our big chance! We'll snatch the girl!'

'Snatch the girl!' gasped the woman. 'What for? Are you nuts?'

'A hostage might force the old man to speak,' murmured Williams. 'And they're headed this way. I'll take care of Boyd. You get the girl straight into this taxi and make for the city. I'll follow by car.'

The footsteps of their unsuspecting quarry rapidly approached, crunching on the gravel of the drive. Williams and Myra crouched back yet further into the shadow of the taxi, and the man, reaching into his pocket, produced a handy rubber cosh. This he gave to Myra, and having armed himself with a similar weapon, waited tensely.

Shirley Duncan and her companion drew level with the taxi and the grim attendant figure sprawled in the drive.

Boyd looked down. 'Poor devil!' he said, and for a moment they paused. In that instant two black shadows detached themselves from the black bulk of the vehicle.

'Ian!' cried Shirley, 'Look out!' But she was too late. The expertly wielded truncheon descended on Boyd's head with sickening force. The sound of the blow was audible in the stillness of the night. The big man sagged like a puppet whose strings have suddenly dropped. He collapsed upon the body of the taxi-man, his white face upturned.

Shirley Duncan turned instinctively to fly. Suddenly she saw before her the dim figure of a woman, her hand upraised.

'No!' she cried, 'No!'

She felt a sickening, numbing impact on her temple. The night suddenly dissolved in fiery particles of flame and whirling discs of light. Then she was falling, falling, falling . . .

* * *

It seemed long, long afterwards that she heard voices and felt some degree of warmth and strength returning to her limbs. She opened her eyes, then shut them fast again as a dreadful spasm of pain possessed her whole head and neck.

A voice said: 'Drink this!' A hand supported her head, and she felt the swift sting of brandy on her lips. Suddenly her stomach burned with the spirit. She coughed, and at length looked up.

A dark-featured man was bending over her, a frown distorting his saturnine features. His black hair was closely brushed and shone with brilliantine, his lean jowl was close shaved.

Marcus Williams said: 'You shouldn't have hit her so hard, Myra.'

Another figure moved into the range of Shirley's vision.

The girl saw a woman of, perhaps, twenty-seven. Her lithe figure suggested great reserves of energy, and her green eyes were utterly hard and unscrupulous. Her regular clean-cut features were spoiled by a permanently mocking smile, and a sudden narrowing of the eyes when, as now, she listened to another's words.

Shirley struggled into a sitting position. She breathed: 'Who — who are you?' She raised a hand to her throbbing head, and regarded them with curiosity, but oddly enough without fear.

Williams replied: 'That doesn't concern you, Miss Duncan. It's what we want that matters.'

'What you — want?'

Williams nodded. 'Your father has a drawing — rather, drawings. We intend to hold you until he surrenders his designs as, shall we say, payment for your ransom?'

Shirley gasped. 'You're Williams!' she said. 'Marcus Williams — and this woman is Myra!'

Myra Williams said: 'How knowledge-able the little darling is and how quickly dear Mr. Boyd blows the gaff!'

'Did Boyd tell you about us?' demanded the man.

'Who else?' asked Myra, 'Santa Claus?' She raised a satirical eyebrow, and Williams blushed hotly.

'Cut it out, Myra!' he said harshly. He turned again to Shirley. 'Get it into your head that it's our intention to hold on to you until your father gives us all the necessary details about this new explosive of his. We intend to set him a clear time limit, and if that expires before he's delivered the goods — well, so much the worse for you, Miss Duncan.'

Shirley Duncan made no immediate reply, then she said, quite deliberately, 'You're wasting your time, both of you. A gang of men attacked the house tonight, and the plans were given to them in exchange for our safety.'

There was a silence, then, 'You're lying!' spat Williams.

Shirley Duncan shook her head. 'It was the plans or the lives of all of us,' she said,

'And Daddy turned over the plans.'

'*He'd* never have done that,' asserted Williams, and for the moment Shirley's eyes flinched before the intensity of his gaze. She felt the colour rising swiftly to her cheeks. Why had she lied so easily to save Ian Boyd's good name? Her heart beat violently, and once more she saw Boyd's pale face staring up at her from where he had fallen under that treacherous blow. Had these devils killed him? Had they?

But before she could frame a question, Williams was speaking again, 'Your tale seems a shade too glib, my dear. But I can soon verify your story. Very soon.' He looked at Myra. 'Make her comfortable, my dear,' he said, 'I'm going to a call box, I want to phone a friend of ours.'

'Larry?' asked Myra.

The man nodded. 'Larry.'

'Some friend!' said Myra Williams, and added an epithet not unskilfully selected from the jargon of the gutter.

★ ★ ★

Myra Williams thoughtfully patted her hair into place with long white fingers. In the other hand she carelessly held a blunt-nosed automatic. Neither woman spoke and after a while Myra rose and paced the room, her green eyes speculative. Never for a moment, however, did she fail to keep the automatic directed towards Shirley, and once when the girl suddenly stirred, she hissed like a snake and brought the weapon up quickly, its blue-steel muzzle shining dully.

'No tricks, now!' she cautioned harshly. The minutes dragged slowly, interminably past. Suddenly, Myra paused in her nervous circuiting of the room, and produced a flat gold case from which she selected a cigarette. Pocketing the case again, she brought out a lighter, snapped on the tiny flame and lit her cigarette with every evidence of satisfaction. Throughout the entire operation she kept her gaze focussed on Shirley Duncan

Shirley said: 'May I have a cigarette?' The throbbing pain at her temple was diminishing a little, now. Myra's carefully pencilled eyebrows arched suspiciously.

'I don't feel too well,' continued Shirley, and she closed her eyes weakly. 'This waiting is very trying, you know.'

Myra laughed coldly. 'Take care you don't meet up with something much more trying than just waiting,' she said ironically, then: 'Catch!'

She extracted the case, and tossed a cigarette to Shirley. The girl caught it and held it for a moment.

'May I have a light?' she asked.

Myra nodded. 'Coming over,' she said and added with heavy sarcasm: 'Don't burn yourself!'

Shirley caught the small silver lighter and flicked the spring-loaded wheel. The flame ate steadily into the white cylinder of the cigarette. She inhaled deeply, and said, 'Thank you!' Simultaneously, she flung the lighter with all her power into Mrya Williams's face and leapt towards her captor, head bent low.

Her shoulder thrust hard into the woman's middle while her hand feverishly sought for the gun. In a split second she had caught the surprised Myra's gun-wrist and had begun to twist the weapon free.

Though she fought spiritedly for her freedom, such a combat was alien to Shirley's nature. Brought up to enjoy a fairly sheltered existence, she had last experienced a rough-and-tumble in her schooldays, and then only of a tomboyish kind, without any real vindictiveness. Certainly she had never once in her life tried to overcome a resolute and vicious adversary.

But within three seconds she was fighting with a savagery that frightened her. Myra recovered quickly from her initial surprise, and from the very considerable pain inflicted when the thrown lighter had struck her forehead. The gun had dropped to the floor, and a kicking foot had shot it beneath a nearby chair. Now, Myra grabbed Shirley's hair with one hand and viciously struck her face with the other. Shirley, fired to an almost primitive anger drove her foot hard against the woman's shin, and had the satisfaction of hearing Myra's grunt of pain. Momentarily, Myra released her hold.

Blindly, Shirley dashed for the door,

but Myra's foot caught hers and she went down. Before she could rise, Myra was on her; her hands clawing and tearing at Shirley's back and neck.

Shirley cried out with pain, and rolled over, kicking as she did. Again, she felt her shoe connect, and heard Myra groan. Then, with photographic clearness, Shirley saw the small black bulk of the automatic lying close by her hand under the low easy chair. She closed her fingers round the butt and drew it towards her.

Myra was now between Shirley and the door, a poker in her hand, picked up from the hearth. Gaspingly she faced the girl, swinging the poker aloft to strike or to throw.

'Put that down!' cried Shirley, 'Or I'll shoot!'

A look of baffled fury overspread Myra's countenance, and she spat out a foul name at Shirley. But the younger girl stood her ground.

Then Myra's expression changed. She grinned derisively and jeered:

'You damned little fool! It isn't loaded!'

Menacingly, she took a step forward,

swinging the poker again, then stopped as Shirley pointed the gun carefully at her chest.

'If you come any nearer I'll find out whether it's loaded or not — by pressing the trigger. Now, put down that poker and stand aside!'

For a second Myra hesitated.

'Get away from that door!' commanded Shirley, 'I'm leaving! Hurry, now!' She was breathing hard, but her tone was even and resolute. She was quite determined to fire unless the woman allowed her to go.

Myra looked at her flushed, determined young face, and knew she was beaten. She threw down the poker and moved over against the wall. Shirley walked steadily towards the door, keeping the small blue-black weapon pointed at Myra. 'Don't try to follow,' she warned, 'Or I shall fire!' She turned the doorknob without taking her eyes from the woman, and stepped out on to the darkened stair head.

Emerging with a feeling of indescribable relief, she shut the door carefully behind her and to her joy saw that the lock held a key. This she turned. She started down the stairs — where they led she did not know — but she descended swiftly, and found herself confronted by what was evidently the street door. It was open!

The street glimmered with the moisture of a recent rainstorm. Away to her left, Shirley could see the glimmering lights of a main thoroughfare, and towards these she now hastened. But before she had negotiated ten yards of the dark side street, she heard a muffled exclamation behind her.

She turned, and saw the tall figure of a man starting towards her — beginning to run. It was Marcus Williams!

Shirley swung the gun in a wide arc, and pressed the trigger. The weapon exploded startlingly, leaping like a live thing in her inexpert grasp. She was conscious of an angry shout, then she was running like a hunted animal!

She made desperately for the beckoning lights of the main street. She heard footsteps swiftly following her. Her lungs began to labour. Every breath seemed to be drawn against some oppressive weight. Her legs and ankles ached as she spurred herself to still greater efforts. The gun clattered from her grasp, but she dared not pause to retrieve it . . .

Then suddenly the bright lights were above her and around her, and almost dead ahead she saw the stationary bulk of a 'bus, its engine throbbing comfortingly. Almost in tears she scrambled, half-fell on to its platform, and even as an astonished conductress grasped her arm, the 'bus jerked forward, accelerated, and she was headed, at last, for safety!

6

Fakes

Twelve hours after Shirley's fight for freedom, Larry Van Grote walked into the garage, which was the joy and pride of Joshua Spellwing's heart. Van Grote's limousine was standing at the sidewalk, Nick Murdoch at the wheel, his face impassive. The Gunner accompanied Larry into the garage, and neither spoke as they climbed the oil-soaked stairs to an office set crazily on the roof. The whole building crouched in the black shadow of a grey stone viaduct, as if hiding from the sun. Spelwing's office was framed by the arch of the viaduct and the garage roof. Trains rumbled overhead at intervals, almost drowning conversation, while from the greasy workshop below sounds of hammering arose.

Outside the office, with its litter of drawings, letters and unpaid bills on a wide desk, sat Spellwing. There was something oddly bestial about him, about his vast untidy bulk and simian features. His eyes only betrayed his native intelligence — and shiftlessness. Black and luminous under the shaggy brows, they confronted the world with an almost impudent stare. Joshua grinned uncertainly at Van Grote and the Gunner, and then gave another glance at the drawings he had pinned before him.

'What do you make of it, Spellwing?' demanded Larry. 'Made a start on the machine yet?'

Spellwing licked his dry, pendulous lower lip. His high-domed forehead wrinkled. All of a sudden sweat glistened on his bald head. He gave a deprecatory smile, and then he spoke in a rush.

'Larry,' he said, 'We've been had. These drawings just don't make sense.'

Larry was selecting a cigarette, and his movements, suddenly became very slow.

'What d'you mean, Spellwing?' he demanded at last. 'You identified them at the Duncan place readily enough. What's the matter now?'

Joshua shrugged. 'Last night I had to work by torchlight, and the plans had every air of genuineness — yes!'

He spread his hands: 'But they're fakes, my friend, fakes drawn by an expert draughtsman from the originals, but with certain integral portions missing. Also, the formula for the thuramite itself is nonsense, a jumble of algebraic signs and figures that lead nowhere!'

Van Grote did not speak, then he said, speculatively: 'I think that ugly face of yours should be changed a little, Joshua.'

The Gunner rose and dropped a hand into his side pocket. He approached Spellwing with a swift, silent tread.

The engineer half rose and sudden terror shone in his eyes. 'Don't!' he cried abruptly, in a voice sharpened by fear almost to a falsetto. Then the Gunner hit him once twice, with the butt of his gun.

Joshua Spellwing dropped to his knees, his hands clawing at his battered face, red threads forcing their slow way between his fingers.

'Okay, Gunner!' said Larry.

A train roared overhead making the

room shudder with the thunder of its passing. The Gunner returned to his seat. Spellwing remained kneeling. The blood was running down his wrists, now, in thin scarlet lines.

'Listen, Spellwing,' said Larry, 'And remember! I don't allow mistakes in my show. You were taken to the Duncan place for the express purpose of identifying those plans — and you failed!' He paused, then went on: 'That business last night cost me a good deal of money and trouble. Now I've got to retrace my steps. Joshua, how long did it take for those fakes to be made ready?'

Spellwing said in a muffled voice: 'About a day,'

'H'm,' muttered van Grote, 'So either Duncan or Boyd had those fakes ready for us when we raided the Duncans' place.'

'Boyd?' queried the Gunner suddenly.

'Yes,' nodded the other, 'He's deeper in this than we think. What he told Morris about just being here to visit the Duncans was bunk.'

Van Grote rose and drew on his gloves.

'Joshua,' he said, 'I'm going to get you those plans and you're going to make my little gadget.' He pointed to the drawing board. 'In the meantime hang on to those pretty pictures. And no more mistakes, Josh, no more mistakes.' He nodded to the Gunner and the two men left the room.

Alone, Joshua Spellwing rocked back on to his heels and began suddenly to weep, helplessly, heartrendingly, like a child.

The Gunner and his chief climbed back into their car, Murdoch let in the clutch and the machine purred smoothly forward. For a while Van Grote sat wrapped in thought, then he said abruptly:

'Boys! We've got to move fast! I'm not the only guy interested in Duncan's contraption. Shirley Duncan was snatched last night.'

Murdoch whistled softly, 'Who — ?' he asked.

'Don't know,' returned Larry Van Grote, 'But whoever it was 'phoned me from a call-box. He fished for information

— plenty. Offered me a cut of whatever information he could get out of old Duncan — for five thousand, cash!' He chuckled coldly. 'And boy! How he wanted to know whether I had those plans or not!'

The Gunner queried: 'And?'

'And I left little boy-blue right in the dark!' said Van Grote.

They were passing through the city centre now, the car weaving in and out of the traffic stream. Murdoch, an expert. getaway man, drove with a vicious skill. Once his mudguards almost caught an elderly woman at a crossing, once he touched fenders with a car ahead.

'Careful!' snarled Larry. 'We don't want to tangle with some fresh traffic cop.'

Murdoch slackened speed.

'Bit touchy after the Duncan House job, chief?' he queried mildly.

'Touchy nothing!' snapped Van Grote. 'There's no positive evidence to link us with that. The police will know all right, but backing up a definite charge is another matter . . . '

He paused, then suddenly cried 'Stop!

Nick, stop this car. Pull over to the kerb.'

Obediently Murdoch edged the limousine up to the sidewalk and stopped, the engine idling. 'Get out and get a paper!' ordered Van Grote, 'Quick!'

Murdoch slid from behind the wheel and vanished. The two men waited.

'Did you hear what that newsboy was shouting at the traffic-halt?' demanded Larry. The Gunner shook his head. 'You should keep your ears open, Gunner!' said Van Grote. 'Your ears open and your mouth shut, always. It's the most sensible way of life.'

Murdoch returned. 'Here,' he said, and handed in a newspaper.

'Okay,' said Van Grote, 'Get going.' He took the paper and quickly scanned its columns. The car moved off again, its hooter bleating.

Van Grote gave a swift gasp of satisfaction. He handed the newspaper to the Gunner, and pointed to a squat black headline. Holding the paper stretched in his hands to reduce the vibration of the car, the Gunner read aloud:

'*MYSTERIOUS AFFAIR IN CITY —*

SCIENTIST'S DAUGHTER MOLESTED.

'Shortly after midnight last night a young woman boarded one of the last city 'buses, in a state of collapse. She was conveyed by ambulance from a police-post to the General Hospital, where she was ultimately identified as Shirley Duncan, the twenty-two year old daughter of Professor Ramsay Duncan, well-known scientist.

Professor Duncan has so far refused to make a statement but our correspondent understands that Miss Duncan was kidnapped by a man and woman who held her captive for some time in a flat near to a local 'bus terminus. A police raid early today on the premises in question failed to reveal any suspects, the kidnappers having apparently fled the building.

When our correspondent attempted to enter the Duncan estate, he was refused admittance, but reports that the whole area appears to have been sealed-off by the police and an extraordinary state — almost of siege — imposed on the neighbourhood.

Shortly before midday today, Professor Duncan and Sir Henry Peterson, the Chief Constable, called at the hospital and after about an hour with Miss Duncan left for an unknown destination.'

'Gee!' said Murdoch, 'did you get that, boss?'

Van Grote nodded.

Murdoch said: 'It's an odd doings, boss, but that job sounds like the Williamses to me. Marcus and Myra Williams. He was once a 'con' man, then went into the 'snatch' racket.' He paused reflectively, and shifted gears. 'He's a handy boy with the explosives, and perhaps he hung that firework on Duncan's car . . . '

'Williams, you say?' queried Van Grote.

'Yep!'

'Can you describe them? Know their habits?'

Murdoch nodded. 'Too well,' he said ironically. 'I once tangled with friend Marcus in Stockholm — he specialises, too, in international jobs — an' I was nearly left holding the baby. Nearly!' he concluded and laughed.

'Right ho!' said Larry, 'Try and look the Williamses up, Nick. I'll foot your account whatever it may be. I want to know just what their game is, and if they're too interested.' He grinned. 'Well, Nick, you can give him the pay-off for Stockholm.'

Murdoch raised a hand from the wheel in a gesture of satisfaction.

The Gunner said, 'How about the Duncans, chief?'

Van Grote smiled thoughtfully.

'I've got an idea, Gunner,' he said at length, 'An idea that might wrap the whole job up at once.' He leaned forward and said to Murdoch, 'Drop us at Ahmed's place, and tell the boys that I'm working from there from now on.'

He retrieved the newspaper from the Gunner and tapped it with a speculative finger.

'Yes, Gunner, I've got a hunch. And it if works out old Duncan's plans are in my pocket.'

7

Open War

At Ramsay Duncan's insistent invitation, Detective-Inspector Boyd was staying at Duncan House as a guest — an arrangement that he would have admitted suited him admirably. For one thing, he was pledged to protect Duncan's drawings, and if possible, to induce him to hand them over to government agents; for another he could now appoint himself permanent escort to Shirley Duncan.

The inventor had not yet reached a decision about the future of his explosive and its detonating machine. Even after realising the significance of Shirley's kidnapping by the Williamses, he could not be brought to see that for his own immediate safety — no less than for that of the country as a whole — he should hand over the secret to Boyd and place himself at the disposal of the Home

Office. With many misgivings therefore, Ian had been forced to hand back the real sheaf of drawings to their rightful owner.

At Duncan House the man from the Yard could see Shirley and enjoy her company almost continually. On the evening of his first day, they walked through the grounds of the mansion and strolled through the surrounding lanes while Shirley Duncan talked charmingly about her younger days and about her hopes for the future.

'I think Daddy will burn his drawings,' she said abruptly as they stared into the small lily-pond on whose surface floated great waxen rafts of the exotic pink-and-white flowers. The evening was growing old, and the dusk was already mantling the trees.

'I wish he would hand them over to the Government,' replied Ian instantly.

Shirley smiled faintly.

'That would solve all our problems, wouldn't it?' she said. 'I agree that it would be the safest way. But Daddy is a great individualist and makes up his own mind in his own way about his inventions

— and this is the greatest of them all, and the most perturbing to him. He stumbled on the compound almost by accident, you know, several years ago. He was not specifically searching for a deadly explosive.'

'Anyway,' said Ian, 'he has a big decision to make. I am rather worried. In the first place, the Williamses are lurking about somewhere awaiting their chance to steal the secret, and you know only too well that a country house is no safe hiding place for such a thing. And Van Grote is a more difficult proposition than even Marcus and Myra. If he has taken that sheaf of drawings to an expert, he knows that they are fakes by now.'

She laughed gleefully, then said: 'Surely we're safe enough, Mr. Boyd. Look at all the policemen you've got in hiding around this house. I found one having a quiet smoke in the summerhouse this morning, and one is hiding behind the hedge near the crossroads all the time!'

'Guardians of the peace,' returned Ian gravely. 'You shouldn't object. As a tax-payer you're receiving some value for your money.'

They went indoors.

Shortly before dinner was due to be served, Ian was invited to join Mr. Duncan in the library. As he entered the room, Boyd noted the grim, set lines around Ramsay Duncan's mouth.

'I have decided to burn the drawings, Inspector.'

'That is quite the wrong way out of your dilemma,' said Ian calmly.

'My decision is final. It is based on principle, not on a personal whim. The world will be better off without this discovery of mine.'

'This is a free country,' said Ian gravely, 'Your drawings are yours to do with as you please.'

Nevertheless, he was worried. He heard Duncan sigh, as though with relief that his mind was at last made up. Then the older man turned to a tall Dutch corner-cupboard, fumbled at the keyplate, and opened the long glazed doors. He reached inside and extracted a silver-covered box and from this thoughtfully withdrew the fateful drawings and the small box of thuramite.

'May I have your cigarette-lighter?' he asked Boyd.

The Home Office man hesitated for a second, then handed the scientist his lighter. Duncan undid the sealed package of drawings, looked at them wistfully, and snapped on the lighter. He moved towards the hearth.

'Get your hands up!' snapped a voice from the doorway. 'Quick! Both of you!'

The two men turned in astonishment. Framed in the doorway stood an odd figure; that of an old man, with a long, ragged moustache and weather-beaten cheeks. On his head was a battered trilby hat, a long, ancient raglan coat draped his form. In his right hand, pointed unwaveringly towards them, they saw a large and purposeful automatic pistol, its blunt muzzle masked by the long cylinder of a maximum silencer. Beneath his left arm, he carried a bundle of evening papers. These now fell to the floor as with a swift, even tread he came forward and clutched at the package in Duncan's hand.

'I want these drawings, thank you,' he said.

In that split second Ian leaped forward. But the man was too swift for him. Pivoting like a trained wrestler, the newcomer struck Ian with all his force on the side of the head with the gun barrel, and Ian dropped, dazed and nauseated, to one knee.

Dimly he heard Duncan's shout of alarm, heard the slam at the library door, and rose groggily to his feet. Duncan was already tugging at the handle of the door. 'Quick! Quick!' cried the scientist, 'He went this way!'

Together they beat on the thick panels of the door, still scarred and splintered from the machine-gun attack of the previous day. But the door held, until with surprising suddenness it opened to disclose the red face of a perspiring policeman.

'Where did that man go?' snapped Ian.

'Who?' asked the bewildered constable.

'The old man — moustache and raglan coat — '

'Oh, the newspaper fellow,' said the constable. 'He went outside, surely, back on his round.'

'Did you let him in?' stormed Ian.

The constable's face was a study in scarlet.

'Why, — I — ' he spluttered. Ian became suddenly aware of Duncan's presence at his elbow. There was a glint of triumph in the older man's eyes. 'He only got half!' said Duncan.

'Half?' queried Ian.

'A portion of the plans!' returned Duncan. 'See!' he held up a number of papers. 'I dropped the rest in the brief moment when you tackled him. Here they are!'

Ian started for the main door.

'Where are you going?' asked the scientist.

'He may only have half your drawings,' said Ian, 'but I'm going to get them back!' A second later the hall door closed behind him, and he was running down the drive.

* * *

Marcus Williams had no time to shed his disguise. He seized the ancient bicycle that had conveyed him to Duncan House, mounted it, and pedalled furiously for where his car was hidden off the main road. He was perhaps halfway down the drive when the bicycle skidded in a patch of gravel and flung him clear. Cursing and wincing with the pain of a badly-scraped hand, he picked up the machine. Then with a gesture of disgust and fury he tossed it away from him. The front wheel was buckled! He began to run.

Perhaps seven minutes later he reached his car, winded and panting. He threw himself into the driver's seat and pressed the self-starter . . .

Even as the car leaped forward, Ian Boyd flung himself onto the rear bumper, found a hold, and clung firmly to the machine which gathered speed and surged forward into the blue-grey of the evening sky, the damp road hissing beneath its flying tyres.

For twenty minutes the car swayed and roared beneath him and he clung desperately to whatever finger hold he could secure. Then, quite suddenly, the car braked to a standstill. He dropped down from his perch, and crouched, waiting. A voice said, insolently:

'Good evening, Inspector!'

He looked up into the levelled revolver and grinning features of Marcus Williams.

He rose slowly to his feet.

'Marcus Williams, I presume?' he exclaimed.

Marcus bowed derisively.

'Himself, Inspector! How did you like my aged newsvendor act?'

'Far too convincing!' admitted Ian grimly.

'Anyway, I got the plans,' said Williams triumphantly, 'And when they leave my hands it will not be in England, but it will be for a large and comfortable sum of foreign currency. I intend to travel and see the world.'

He was about to turn and go, when Boyd asked him:

'But how did you know that Van Grote had failed to get the real stuff?'

'Simple!' said Marcus. 'I knew that Van Grote was in close contact with old

Spellwing, the Mad Mechanic as they used to call him in the forged currency racket. Spellwing made the best phoney plates for counterfeit-printing ever known in the business. And when I heard that Van Grote had got him up here I knew it was for,' his mouth wrinkled wryly, 'for no honest business!' He laughed. 'So I looked Spellwing up, and he told me that Larry had already been to him — had in fact taken him out to the Duncan House on his mob's last visit there to identify the plans. Larry had been no end annoyed when he'd discovered himself landed with a pack of duds and had taken it out on the Mechanic. Spellwing was as mad as a snake at him and spilled the beans to me while nursing a damaged face. Well, goodbye.'

'No shooting?' said Ian.

'No shooting,' returned Marcus. 'Why should I? I don't intend to have a murder rap hanging over me even on the continent. I might have to come back sometime.' He reached for the offside door handle. 'Oh, and I wouldn't be at all surprised if Larry decided to take

Duncan House apart again tonight,' he said, 'He always was a quick worker. So long!'

He leaped into the driving seat, and the car jerked forward. The last words he heard from Williams were shaped into an ironic farewell:

'Don't walk your legs down to the knees, Inspector. Try for a lift. I'd take you into town, but I'm going places!'

The car quickly vanished into the gloom, leaving Boyd staring angrily after it.

★ ★ ★

Van Grote's henchmen arrived with their leader at Duncan House in two supercharged cars. The leafy wood that swallowed the vehicles was not too far from their objective and yet not so near as to give premature warning to the police patrolling the estate. Their engines throbbed into silence, headlights blacked-out, the eight men gathered into a cluster, speaking in monosyllables. Each man was armed, one with a tommy-gun.

They might have been respectable city men setting off to a dance or a dinner. They wore well-cut gabardine raincoats and soft hats. One sported a fine silk neckerchief. They buttoned their coats up to the chin and set out at a single word of command from Van Grote, who now adjusted a thin black mask to his face as did Nick.

Van Grote and his lieutenant walked with the machine-gunner and one other man. The Gunner commanded the rearguard. They crossed the road into the cover of the hedges, and a man stumbled and cursed. Otherwise they made no sound. Suddenly, they came upon the greystone wall encircling the Duncan estate. One by one they mounted it, and slipped like wraiths into the shadows of the trees.

So far they had eluded the police patrols, but now, as they moved silently through the deep gloom, a police officer walked suddenly and unsuspectingly into them.

For one second the man stood still in surprise, then he half-raised his whistle to his lips. As he did so, Larry Van Grote shot him through the heart.

The silenced pistol made little more sound than a single tap upon a kettledrum. Nick stepped forward and caught the toppling body, easing it gently to the ground. Silently he rejoined Van Grote and the machine-gunner, and they moved forward again, following Van Grote's plan of attack, which was to come as quietly as possible up to the house, then to force an entrance by one of the ground floor windows, disposing of any opposition ruthlessly. In an emergency, the sound of firing was to signal a general rush upon the house.

This was, in fact, what occurred. Two policemen suddenly appeared directly ahead through the bushes, slowly patrolling the driveway. They were young men, swift and alert, and the sharp snapping of a stick drew the attention of one of them. As they turned into the bushes to investigate, Van Grote signalled sharply to the tommy-gunner.

The weapon broke into a shattering-fusillade of sound and the two policemen went over like ninepins, unable to reach their holstered guns before death took them.

'Come on!' yelled Van Grote, 'Make for the house!'

He broke into a run, closely followed by Nick, heading for the dim bulk of the house which now lay directly ahead. Lights flicked suddenly on in the windows. They heard a door open and close, and a man shouted. Then they were upon the house itself, and Nick smashed at the glass of the great window with the butt of his gun. He slipped his hand inside and undid the catches.

Van Grote entered immediately after Nick, the tommy-gunner following. They paused momentarily, blinded by the bright lights of the hall. Four more men thrust into the hall through the open window. The remaining man was to stay outside, covering their proposed line of retreat.

Suddenly, from the head of the stairway two explosions rang out almost simultaneously and the knot of mobsters scattered precipitately, all except one, who with a sharp, dreadful scream flung up his arms and crumpled to the floor in a spreading pool of crimson.

Automatically, the machine-gunner raised his weapon and fired. There came a cry of agony, and down the stairway lurched the body of Duncan's elderly butler, a shotgun tumbling from his dying hands.

'This way!' shouted Van Grote, running for the library doors.

He flung his full weight against them — but they were secured inside, and he recoiled, grasping a numbed shoulder. 'Smash it in!' he commanded.

Two men flung their combined weight against the door and the lock gave way abruptly. For a split second the two thugs staggered in the doorway, framed in the bright square of light. Then the harsh thunder of an automatic filled the library. One of Van Grote's hirelings spun like a top, his face suddenly a mask of blood. He crashed to the floor head foremost, like a swimmer diving into a pool. The other screamed an oath and staggered back, clutching his shoulder.

Again the rattle of the tommy-gun rang out, as Van Grote's machine-gunner sprayed the inside of the library blindly from his position in the hallway.

'We're coming in,' yelled Van Grote savagely. 'Heaven help you if you shoot again.'

He entered the room at a run, closely followed by Nick. The atmosphere was foul with cordite fumes. On the floor lay the body of Ramsay Duncan, a pool of blood encircling his head. Shirley Duncan stood looking down at him with horror written pallidly upon her features.

'You've killed my father!' she shrieked.

Blindly, she tried to advance towards them, but nausea claimed her and she stood swaying, her hand over her eyes as if to shut out the incredible scene.

'Where's that drawing?' snapped Van Grote. Then his expression changed to one of triumph. He rushed to the desk and picked up the thuramite box and a sheaf of papers. 'This is it, Nick!' he said thickly, scanning the drawings. 'Right to hand, all nice and neatly packed up ready for us! What could have been better?'

'Let's get going, boss,' advised the other, moistening his lips. 'Is it the goods, this time?'

'Yes!' declared Van Grote, 'It's a hundred-to-one they wouldn't have two sets of fakes. And anyway, here's the stuff with it!' He held up the box triumphantly, 'These are the plans all right.'

He thrust the papers into a specially-made inside pocket, over which he buttoned a linen flap. The box he put carefully into his trouser-pocket.

'Right-ho, Nick! We're on our way! Bring the girl and let's get back to the cars!'

'The girl?' Nick queried incredulously.

'The girl!' assented Van Grote. 'She'll stop any odd coppers firing after us, and she may be a useful hostage. Come on, you — get moving!'

Nick seized Shirley's right arm and Van Grote her left. Together they hurried her towards the door.

8

The Hideout

Van Grote's two cars entered the city by separate, devious ways; but their destination was the same — a tumbledown garage in an insalubrious street a few blocks from Spellwing's place.

Van Grote was deep in thought. his head sunk on his broad shoulders. He stood in the dingy garage while outside an innocent-seeming taxi waited with chugging engine to hurry the members of his gang to their next — and final — hideout.

He said at last: 'Anybody who says we raided Duncan House tonight is making a mistake. There are other mobs in this town! Anyway, I'm fixing alibis for the lot of us right now — and it'll cost a pretty penny, I assure you. Better play safe. Nobody could have recognised us, but dead cops raise a helluva row in this country. I think we'd better lie low until

Sankey fixes the alibis.'

Nick asked, 'Where do we go? Not to Ritter's filthy dive, I hope?'

Van Grote shook his head. 'No. I've got a new fellow who can put us up for weeks on end if need be. It all depends on how quickly Spellwing can get the machine ready for me, and how quickly Druten can lay in chemicals enough to fix the other end of the job. The stuff might want some special material that isn't too easily obtainable without raising suspicion.' He made a gesture as of dismissal. 'That's the set-up, anyway. Once we're fixed for the big job, Nick, we'll find a place in the country, and that'll become headquarters.'

Nick nodded quietly. The Gunner said nothing. The other hirelings were little bothered by anything they heard — phlegmatic and unquestioning as they were, they thought only of the abundant resources Van Grote controlled, and with which (when the mood took him) he could be surprisingly generous.

Shirley Duncan, gagged, her wrists secured with adhesive tape, was inside one of the big limousines. Ted Morris her sometime amiable escort, had bound her wrists before the car had left Duncan House, and had forced his silk scarf into her mouth without compunction, stifling her cries.

The thronging images that flashed across the screen of her mind were vivid and horrible. One thought dominated all others: her father was dead, brutally murdered! Murdered! It seemed incredible — a memory born out of some nightmare, not real. Yet she knew all too well that it was true!

She had lost the father she adored.

Vaguely she began to wonder what Van Grote intended to do with her. The men had unmasked now, and she had been able to study the face of the gang leader, the face of the man she now hated more than any other in the world. Van Grote was so obviously a leader among these men — swift, ruthless, and without pity.

She wondered what Van Grote's reaction would be when he learned that he had obtained only one half of the drawings of the detonating device. And she thought about Ian. Had he caught the bogus newsvendor? If he retrieved the other half of the drawings, it would be wisdom to destroy it. But what if Ian had been unlucky?

Her reflections were cut short by the appearance of Ted Morris who bundled her roughly out of the car. He removed the gag almost as violently as he had applied it earlier.

'You're going with us now,' he said, 'but don't try to shout. Van Grote will give you hell if you make a scene.'

She had little chance to scream, however. She was hurled into the taxi with the others and the vehicle moved away, in what direction Shirley did not know. She sat between Van Grote and Ted Morris, with two gunmen facing her. Nick and the Gunner occupied the driving compartment with Nick behind the wheel.

* * *

Down by the river, among an agglomeration of houses that seemed to have their foundations in the very riverbed, there stood the house of Ahmed Fey, and to his tall rambling abode Nick drove the taxi.

The door, set in a pool of shadow at the bottom of a flight of crumbling stone stairs leading to some mysterious basement, opened swiftly to Van Grote's single knock. Already they had been observed through a peephole.

Inside Ahmed Fey was waiting for them. He wore a dirty white robe caught up loosely with a girdle at the waist, and a greasy tarboosh. His dusky, aquiline features were set in their habitual grin, a sign of pleasure belied by the cold glint in his deep-set eyes.

Ahmed bowed to Van Grote, and without speaking turned and led the party down a tortuous, dim-lit passage way. A door was thrown open. Shirley was thrust into a windowless apartment, more closely resembling a cellar or cavern than a room. She gazed fearfully at the dirty bed and broken chair.

Van Grote was haggling with Ahmed Fey.

'We want to cover up for a week, maybe

less. If the cops come along, we don't want to be found. What's your price?'

''Price?' repeated Ahmed, and he spread his hands. 'The price is fifty pounds each man.'

Van Grote snarled in his face.

'Why, you dirty-looking devil.'

Ahmed Fey was patient.

'The police — they cannot find you here,' he said. 'They do not often come, for it is always the same, nobody here to find. I can hide you, Mister Grote, and we have some very good card games, eh? Fifty pounds each man, and for the woman — yes?'

Van Grote replied, 'I'll pay you your three hundred and fifty, but you're due for hell if you fail me. Me and my boys will pull you to bits.' He paused, then added, 'Show me where we hide out, and it had better be good.'

Ted Morris joined the others at that moment.

'This is a dump!' he said disgustedly.

'If you don't like it, you can skip out,' said Van Grote softly. 'It's costing me fifty quid to keep you here for a week.'

Ted shrugged.

In this incredible rabbit-warren of a house there were many passages, all studded with locked doors. Ahmed Fey took the men through windowless corridors to three rooms at the end of a passage. Inside the accommodation was surprisingly good. The rooms were bedrooms, neatly and simply furnished.

Ahmed Fey began to describe the routine to them.

'I have very good cook and you do only ring for meals and they will be brought to you. Later, I will show you my room where we gamble. You like card-playing?'

'How do we get out of here if the cops rush in?' demanded Van Grote, practically.

'There is a door in each room,' said Ahmed, indicating a second door in the wall of Van Grote's room with a wave of a grimy, skinny hand. 'They all open into a passage and at the end of the passage there is another door, but it is very hard to find, I will show you. Come!'

He showed them in the next few minutes how the three separate rooms had exits into a passage, which in turn had a hidden door. The secret door was a large slab of stone, which pivoted when a concealed spring was operated. Behind the secret door was yet another passage and this led into a disused and forgotten sewer. Here Ahmed stopped.

'Full of rats,' muttered Ted Morris. 'Where does the sewer go?'

'You will never need to leave your rooms,' said Ahmed, and he shook his aged head. 'The police have never found your rooms yet, and they have been here one, two perhaps three times. I put carpet and tables and chairs over the trapdoor which leads down to this floor.'

'Okay,' said Van Grote calmly. 'We'll squat here for a week. By that time Sankey will have alibis fixed for us so that no cop can dare say we weren't in the place Sankey says we were.'

Ahmed Fey nodded his head. They returned to one of the three furnished rooms. Without blinking an eyelid, Ahmed Fey held out his hand.

'My money — please?'

Van Grote did not answer. He brought

a thick notecase into view very slowly. He peeled off one hundred pounds in notes and put them into Ahmed Fey's hand.

'You'll get the rest later.'

The bright black eyes of Ahmed flickered and then he seemed to accept the position.

'You can send your cook in with some grub,' stated Van Grote. 'I guess the fellers are hungry. Bring it here. This is my room, and Nick will sleep here. You other guys can sort yourselves out in the other rooms.'

'Okay, Mr. Van Grote,' lisped Ahmed, and as he moved away, 'you will play cards soon, eh?'

'Anything to pass the time away in this dump,' muttered Ted Morris.

'Count me out,' said Jack the Gunner coolly. 'I'm nobody's pigeon.'

Soon a slightly built, half-caste youth laid a table in Van Grote's room, and the gangsters swiftly disposed of the food prepared for them. An electric fire was switched on and the gang leader drew up a chair and carefully brought the sheaf of drawings from his pocket. He began to study them, frowning in concentration.

Van Grote was a shrewd man, but there were limitations to his knowledge. The figures and tracings before him were absolutely meaningless to him. True, he spent some time studying them, but he learned little from the information printed at the bottom of each quarto page. There were headings and other printed words at the top and bottom of each page, but the import of these he did not understand

As he flicked the pages, he frowned. When the fake drawings had been brought to him after the first raid on Duncan House, he knew there had been twelve pages in the sheaf. And though Spellwing had pronounced them as meaningless fakes, there had been *twelve* pages!

Van Grote flicked through the pages in his hands. He counted seven.

He raised his eyes and stared at the element of the electric fire. Why should the fake drawings have contained twelve pages, if the real drawings comprised only seven?

'This stuff is genuine,' he muttered. 'But there's still something screwy here.'

He rose. He would see the girl before sending the drawings over to Spellwing to work on.

9

I've been Waiting for You!

Van Grote opened the door of Shirley's prison and walked in. He closed the door after him very carefully, and brought out a gun. He did not think for one moment the scared girl would force him to use it, but a gun always made a certain impression. Shirley backed against the wall as he entered.

Van Grote waved the sheaf of drawings.

'How many pages are there here, my dear?' he rapped. 'Come along, you must know?'

She hesitated, wondering what answer he expected. She decided that silence was the best defence.

'The fakes contained twelve pages,' continued Van Grote. He eyed the girl steadily. 'This lot has only seven. How come?'

Still she made no reply.

'You know I could make you talk,' said Grote grimly. 'You little fool! You would talk within ten seconds if I wanted to make you!'

Shirley flinched involuntarily, and he laughed.

'You're lucky,' he sneered. 'I've got a tender spot for the ladies. Anyway, Spellwing will soon give me the lowdown on these drawings.'

He left her, locking the door on the outside.

He returned to his room to find that the Gunner, Ted Morris and the other two mobsters had gone to their respective rooms. Only Nick Murdoch lolled in a chair, staring at the bright red electric fire. The room was stuffy, its atmosphere thick and oppressive.

'There doesn't seem to be much ventilation in this dump,' Van Grote grumbled. He moved over to the bellpush and pressed it.

They waited and eventually the half-caste boy appeared. He looked inquiringly at Van Grote. The gang leader rose slowly and went over to the boy. He gripped the youth's arm suddenly and gave it a vicious wrench. The boy squirmed in sudden pain while his eyes rolled in fear.

'Next time a ring comes from these rooms,' said Van Grote gently, 'jump to it! I don't like to be kept waiting. Tell Ahmed Fey I wanta see him — an' quick!'

The boy fled.

Nick Murdoch did not stir.

Van Grote's threat had some effect for Ahmed came along the passage and knocked with his peculiar double-rap on Van Grote's door. He had not wasted much time.

'I want a message sent to Joshua Spellwing,' Van Grote said, thinking swiftly, then added, 'In fact I want Spellwing brought to me. He'll come. He's working for me.'

'I have a telephone,' said Ahmed Fey. 'While you could not use it, I could send this man Spellwing a message.'

'Send a man instead,' rapped Van Grote. 'It's safer. And I want Spellwing to come here. Do you get me? I don't just want to talk to him.'

'It will take a little time,' muttered the other. 'You understand I am very anxious for your safety while you are my guests. So it will take time to find this Joshua Spellwing and bring him here without the police shadowing him to my door.'

'All right, all right, I understand. I don't want the cops either. Just get Spellwing for me. And here's another job. I want a note sent to Morton Sankey. He's my lawyer. Wait — I'll write you this note. You can find some safe go-between who'll take it to Sankey.'

Van Grote brought a compact notebook from his pocket, ripped two pages from it and began to scribble, finally signing his name with a flourish.

'Make sure your messenger is not picked up,' rapped Van Grote, and he gave the man the note and the addresses of Sankey and Spellwing.

Ahmed Fey shuffled away to carry out his instructions. Nick Murdoch waited until he had disappeared.

'You going to start Spellwing on the machine right now, boss?' he asked.

Van Grote was slow in replying.

119

'There's something damned queer about those papers, Nick. Those fakes ran to twelve pages, but this lot has only seven. I never noticed the difference until I had time to examine them. I want to know why there are only seven pages in this drawing and twelve in the fakes. So I've sent for Spellwing.'

'We're trusting that bird a lot,' observed Nick.

'He likes to live, Nick. I've promised him some dough when he gets this machine of Duncan's built and a quantity of the explosive made.'

'Sooner the better,' said Nick. 'The more I think of it, the more I know it's the hottest scheme ever thought of. You'll be Boss of this city.'

Whether Nick's flattery was deliberate or not, Van Grote liked the sound of it. The picture of Van Grote, virtual dictator of a huge city appealed to his imagination of which he had plenty. His name would fill the world's headlines. And if this town did not like being blackmailed, he would blow half of it to fragments and then concentrate on London, with the fate of this city as a warning. If the police arrived at his headquarters to pick him up he would threaten to blow a section of the city to bits by means of a time switch operating the control.

The payoff would be enormous!

Liking the subject, he talked for the next twenty-five minutes to Nick Murdoch, elaborating various points in his scheme. He even brought out his notebook and scribbled tentative plans and suggestions. Nick listened wisely.

Their conversation was broken by Ahmed Fey's signal knock on the door. Ahmed entered, bringing Joshua Spellwing with him.

'All right, Ahmed, you can go. Spellwing, take a chair.'

Joshua Spellwing sat nervously on the very edge of a chair.

'My messenger take your note safely to Mr. Sankey,' said Ahmed Fey. He walked softly to the door, opened it and went out.

When they were alone, Van Grote brought out the drawings. He thrust them towards Spellwing.

'Look at them. Give me the lowdown — quick! Are they genuine?' He paused. 'Are they *all* there?'

The engineer frowned as he scanned the drawings. He turned over the pages slowly allowing several minutes to each page. Grote said nothing, but intently watched Spellwing's face. Nick Murdoch eyed them both speculatively. He was wondering if Van Grote would ever slip up! He did not think it would be for a long time — probably never once he had the wonder explosive in his hands.

When Spellwing came to the last page of the sheaf of drawings, he glanced sharply up at Van Grote.

'Where is the remainder of the drawings?' he asked

Van Grote hardly moved, but Nick Murdoch saw him tense.

'It's complete, isn't it?' said Van Grote softly.

Spellwing swallowed.

'It can't be. The fakes were drawn on twelve pages.'

'Say, listen, don't you know your job? These are the genuine drawings.'

Van Grote waited for the man's next words.

'They're genuine drawings,' admitted Spellwing. 'But they deal mostly with the firing element and a new and very ingenious radio-control. The machine can't be complete however, without the electrical and coil systems. You must have a metal shell with suitable dimensions and — '

Van Grote jumped to his feet. He was livid with fury.

'Damn that girl! I'll knock the truth out of her. She must know where they are!'

Angrily he made for the door, beckoning Spellwing and Nick to follow him.

Van Grote re-entered Shirley's room like the very angel of terror. He went straight up to the trembling girl and seizing her by the shoulders, shouted: 'I want to know how many sheets your father's drawings actually contained.' He shook her. 'Are you going to talk or have I got to use force?'

At the mention of her father, Shirley broke into tears. Never would she forget the horrible moment when her father had fallen to the library floor, blood streaming from his head.

Van Grote seized her wrist and with all his force twisted her arm. He forced a cry from her lips, but that was all. She struggled and kicked, in a sudden bout of anger, wishing she could kill the man. Van Grote released her, stepped back, and rapped to Nick:

'Grab her! I'll make her tell the truth!'

Nick Murdoch advanced and forced the struggling girl's arms behind her back. Studiously Van Grote brought out an ugly knuckle-duster from his pocket and slipped it on to his hand. He bunched his fist, and raised it to the girl's face.

'This little toy will make a mess of your face, my dear,' he said grimly. 'Now, come clean, or I'll let you have it. I want to know how many sheets this drawing is supposed to contain. I want the truth. Where is the rest of the drawing? Start talking now!'

She faced him completely unafraid. Could her defiance have brought her father to life, Shirley would have suffered torture before she uttered a word.

Nevertheless the girl's brain was working furiously. Van Grote suspected that the drawing was incomplete. In his first attempt to steal her father's invention, he had been thwarted by the fake drawings cleverly prepared by Ian Boyd. Now the gang leader had again been cheated of his purpose. He had only half the drawings!

The newsvendor had the other half — unless Ian had succeeded in retrieving the stolen drawings — and she was certain that *he* was Marcus Williams or his agent.

Therefore if Marcus Williams had the other half of the drawings, what better plan than to set Van Grote pursuing the adventurer? Even if Ian had recovered the other half of the papers, it would be a satisfactory trick to occupy Van Grote's attention with Marcus.

'I'll talk,' she said slowly. 'If you must know, you are not very clever, Mr. Van Grote. You should have twelve pages, as you suspect. The other five pages are in the possession of a man, Marcus Williams!'

She was watching Spellwing's face as she spoke. At the mention of Marcus's name, he trembled and a fine dew of perspiration overspread his forehead. Shirley watched him curiously.

Shirley guessed that the man who trembled so obviously when Marcus William's name was spoken was Spellwing. She knew he was not one of the six gangsters who had brought her to this cellar. Now she wondered what prompted his fear. Illumination suddenly burst upon her. Spellwing knew Williams. Were *they* accomplices, too?

'I've heard that name before,' said Van Grote with a scowl. 'Who is this guy Williams? Don't try to lie or by Heaven I'll make you pay for it!'

'Why should I lie?' she returned. 'I don't want to feel that knuckleduster, Mr. Van Grote. I tell you Marcus Williams got into the library at Duncan House just before you and your men arrived. Williams had a gun and he snatched the drawings from my — my — father's hand.' Shirley paused, a lump in her throat in spite of her determination to tell

126

her story calmly. 'But he — he — was too hasty and only managed to obtain the last pages. Inspector Boyd was with us, and he gave chase, but before he could return, you arrived.'

Van Grote said carefully, 'I want to hear more about this Marcus Williams? Who is he?'

'Some sort of adventurer — A crook! He runs in close harness with a woman called Myra, who passes as his wife. He is after the secret of my father's invention.'

'Is that so?' Van Grote laughed nastily. But he was beginning to look worried. 'So a guy named Marcus Williams has the other five pages! Spellwing, you can stay here tonight and make a tracing of the pages I hold. You can work all night. Then you can get started on as much of the machine as you can make from your tracing. By the time the first parts are ready, I'll have those five pages and a guy named Marcus Williams will be rubbed out — and a dame called Myra!'

'You're in hiding here, aren't you?' inquired Shirley sweetly. 'I daresay that will handicap your search for Marcus

Williams. By now, he might be a hundred miles away.'

'I'll get him so long as he is in the country,' grated Van Grote.

'Why don't you ask Spellwing about Marcus Williams?' Shirley blurted out.

Joshua Spellwing's mouth jerked open. All the blood drained from his face, leaving it ghastly white.

Van Grote's eyes narrowed.

'What is it, Spellwing?'

The engineer said hoarsely: 'She is simply talking rot. I don't know anything about this Williams!'

'I can see you're a blasted liar,' said Van Grote evenly.

Spellwing began to sweat. He swallowed several times and then decided to tell the truth. Van Grote was a swine. He would find out the truth anyway, but he, Spellwing, was valuable. Van Grote could not easily dispense with his services if he wanted Duncan's plans translated into reality.

'I — I — should have told you, Van Grote. A man calling himself Marcus Williams got me alone in my office. He

128

had followed you to my place, he said. He wanted the drawing. He knocked me about. I — I told him your drawing was a fake — just to get rid of him — Van Grote — '

'So he beat me to it,' said Van Grote heavily. 'He got to Duncan's house before me.'

'He would have killed me — ' began Spellwing uneasily.

'And a damned good thing, too! Why didn't you tell me about this guy, you fool?'

Spellwing stammered for words, then lapsed into silence.

'Get on with those tracings!' sneered Van Grote. 'When you leave this place, you'll have a bodyguard, so that you won't be so helpless in future. I'll send Bob Holt out with you. He'll watch out for Williams and if he runs into him — ' He clicked his tongue, ' — It'll be curtains for Williams.'

'I hope you find him,' Shirley taunted.

Van Grote, on his way to the door, half-turned.

'When Williams reads the papers in the

morning he'll soon guess who has the other half of the drawings. Then he'll come to me. Anyway, we'll meet.'

They went, leaving Shirley alone in her cellar-prison. She wondered if she had done the right thing to put Van Grote on Marcus Williams's track, but knew that in this instance thieves would undoubtedly fall out! — with disastrous consequences to one, if not both of them!

She wondered what Van Grote intended to do with her. She was not much use as a prisoner, though the thought suddenly struck her: unless Ian Boyd gained possession of the papers from Marcus Williams. Then, if Van Grote learned of this, she would be a valuable hostage.

Shirley nearly groaned aloud. She heartily wished the papers had never existed. The drawings had brought only disaster and misfortune so far to all who had touched them.

In another room Joshua Spellwing was inwardly wishing he had never seen Van Grote or the Duncan drawings. He had obtained some tracing paper through the medium of Ahmed Fey and with a newly sharpened pencil, he worked industriously, copying the minute lines from seven separate quarto sheets. His domed head glistened with perspiration. Van Grote and Nick Murdoch watched him incuriously. Ted Morris and the other mobsters were somewhere in Ahmed Fey's gambling den. The Gunner was asleep in another room.

Van Grote had intended to keep one eye on Spellwing, and Nick Murdoch, as an industrious lieutenant, stayed with him.

Once Van Grote rang the bell for the half-caste boy and ordered a large supply of black coffee. When it arrived he made Spellwing drink copiously — not that the engineer was reluctant. Indeed, he felt the need of something invigorating. The light in the cellar was bad, and the air stuffy. More than once Spellwing felt so sleepy that he actually nodded as he studied one part of the drawings.

It was early morning when he finally finished the drawings. His haggard face was sprouting a stubble of beard, and there were lines of fatigue under his eyes.

Van Grote had gone to sleep, leaving Nick Murdoch to watch the engineer. Nick rose, yawned and stretched out a hand for the original drawings.

'Finished?' he asked. 'If so, the boss wants these drawings.' Van Grote awakened at the sound of their voices. Within a few seconds his brain was working quickly.

'I'll have to risk Bob Holt,' he said. 'He'll go with Spellwing and keep a lookout for Williams. I'm not worrying about that guy. With only five sheets of the drawing, he can't do much. I'll get into contact with him.'

'What about the cops, boss?'

'Sure, they'll be looking for us, but I can't help that. The special from Scotland Yard will be pretty sore now that Ramsay Duncan is dead and we've got the girl. We'll hang on to the dame just in case the cops get this Williams guy before we do. She'd make a good hostage — good enough to exchange for five sheets of paper.'

Van Grote laughed harshly. He felt suddenly irritable. He wished he was back in his Hope Street flat with every civilized amenity to hand. He scowled.

'Get hold of Bob Holt and tell him what he has to do,' he ordered. 'Then get Ahmed Fey to show them some safe way out to Spellwing's garage. An', Spellwing, don't go to bed. I want those parts as quick as you can make 'em. I might get the other sheets quick. I'm going to think of some scheme to contact Marcus Williams.'

It was some fifteen minutes later that Joshua Spellwing and Bob Holt emerged from the disused sewer that ran from Ahmed Fey's house and came out among the rubble of a derelict brickyard. Spellwing had the tracings. Van Grote was retaining the originals, thus taking no risks of losing the drawings again. Spellwing felt dog-tired, but the fresh air had some effect in bracing him.

The two men walked warily through a few nondescript streets and finally found a taxi. They gave the driver his instructions, then leaned back and brought out cigarettes.

'Van Grote expects a man to work

night and day,' grumbled Spellwing.

'And you'd better do it,' was the uncompromising reply.

Bob Holt was a stocky type with little intelligence. His thin lips made only a narrow line in his face. His blue eyes were devoid of humour.

The taxi finally drew up outside Spellwing's garage, Bob Holt glancing carefully along both sides of the street before descending. Once on the pavement, his movements were quick, spasmodic. He dismissed the driver and he and Spellwing hurried into the garage.

Wearily they climbed the stairs to Spellwing's office. No men were yet on duty in the garage below, and Spellwing switched on a light as he entered his office and made straight for a chair into which he sank with a sigh.

A sharp command rang out —

'Get your hands up!'

Ian Boyd emerged from his hiding place between the filing cabinet and a stand draped with dingy overalls, his gun held ready. Spellwing rose to his feet in terror, at last thoroughly unnerved by this new development.

'Who are you?' he screamed.

Boyd smiled.

'I regret that I cannot give you my card, Mister Spellwing. But if you must know, I am the proverbial man from Scotland Yard.'

Spellwing gave a croak of terror and collapsed into his chair.

In that split second, Bob Holt acted. His automatic was half raised as Ian Boyd fired, twice. The room rang with the metallic uproar of the two explosions. The impact of the heavy bullets thrust Holt back as though he had been struck by a giant, invisible fist. He sagged through the open door, his pistol falling from his nerveless hand. The body sprawled on to the landing, rolled to the top of the stairs, and plunged down out of sight.

Then Spellwing fainted.

10

The Raid

Spellwing slowly recovered consciousness. He saw Ian Boyd bending over him and groaned. Ian said, 'Now I think you'd better talk. Where is Shirley Duncan? Where is Van Grote?'

Spellwing's first few words were almost inaudible. He could hardly control his voice.

'Van Grote is . . . at . . . Ahmed Fey's . . . house . . . down . . . on the river . . . God! He forced me to work for him, I swear it! Grote has the girl there in a cellar . . . '

'I don't know anything about Ahmed Fey,' said Ian grimly, 'But I have friends at Police Headquarters who will soon find out something.'

Spellwing felt the tracings in his inside jacket pocket and the remembrance of them terrified him. He was implicated with Van Grote. Van Grote! The big shot! *But the police were bigger!*

Spellwing's hands trembled. He wished he could take the tracings out of his pocket and make them vanish into thin air.

He decided to confess everything to the big man before him.

'I have some tracings of the pages Van Grote stole from Duncan House,' he babbled. 'I am supposed to start work on the machine right away. Van Grote still has the original drawings, and a small box of the powder.'

'Hand the tracings over,' said Ian curtly.

Spellwing eagerly obeyed. Suddenly the sound of police-car engines came to their ears. Looking out of the window Ian saw a patrol car and an ambulance for which he had telephoned draw into the garage entrance.

A few minutes later, after photographs had been taken, the body of the gangster was taken away and Spellwing accompanied Ian Boyd to the Police Headquarters.

Spellwing was only too ready to make a statement.

Later he would be taken to the cells to be brought up before the magistrates in the morning. The charge, so far, was that he was found in possession of tracings of drawings known to be stolen.

★ ★ ★

Ian Boyd joined the squad of police detailed to raid Ahmed Fey's premises. The men were under the charge of Detective-Inspector MacDonald, of the local C.I D. Ian Boyd sat with the burly detective-inspector in the police patrol car.

'Wily old devil, this Ahmed Fey,' commented MacDonald as the cars set out. 'We know he has a hand in many criminal activities, but so far we have been unable to pin anything definite on him. Those gaming parties of his, for example. The last time we raided him, we couldn't find one damned gambler on the premises. The rotten part was we had a special man who had paid for an invitation to the gaming party, but he disappeared with the rest. Later he was picked out of the river — dead.'

The car turned from the main street across a wide bridge and Ian momentarily glimpsed the steel-grey surface of the river through the steel-lattices.

'The place is a rabbit-warren,' continued the other. 'These men just alter their buildings to suit themselves. They knock walls down, construct passages — Lord knows what!'

The police cars stopped alongside Ahmed Fey's gaunt building and policemen poured out. Some ran immediately round to the back of the house, traversing a narrow alley that resembled a tunnel, its archways crossing above their heads. Evidently these stone bridges were so constructed for the purpose of bracing the adjacent buildings. They took up their positions silently covering the rear of the building.

Detective-Inspector Ian Boyd entered with MacDonald by the main door, which opened at last to his imperative knocking. Ian had been itching to knock the panels in.

'By now everyone in the damned building knows there is a raid on,' he muttered.

They brushed past the half-caste who opened the door, and tramped with their escort swiftly down into the gloomy passages. Ian darted ahead, easing out his police-automatic. He intended to shoot first if he saw anyone with a gun, and to ask questions later. He had spied a staircase leading down to another floor, and running ahead clattered swiftly down the stairs. At the bottom he came face to face with a tall, shrivelled man in a dark suit, whom he instinctively guessed to be Ahmed Fey. Ian grabbed him. One thing he was thankful for; he was a special agent and not under local orders. Ian gripped Ahmed's shoulder, and saw pain and hatred flash suddenly through the man's brown eyes.

'Where is the girl Van Grote brought here?' he asked.

'I do not know,' said Ahmed Fey sibilantly. 'I do not know Van Grote. He is not here.' Ian flung him to one side in disgust.

A clatter of footsteps behind him caused him to turn to face Detective-Inspector MacDonald.

'Will he talk?' inquired the detective-inspector.

'I could make him,' said Ian unpleasantly. 'But if we find nothing, he could hire a good lawyer and I'd be hauled over the coals myself!'

They left Ahmed Fey standing, and plunged along the passage. Two uniformed policemen came down to help in the search. Room doors were wrenched open, but failed to indicate the presence of Van Grote and his men. The passage was evidently well below ground for the walls were damp, and electric light was the only illumination. In one part the brickwork was obviously new. The tunnel, it was little less, twisted crazily. They came across a kitchen and Ahmed Fey's private rooms. The latter were dirty and yet richly furnished in an exotic eastern style. In the kitchen, Ian eyed grimly the cowering boy who shook his head mutely when asked a question.

Ian rejoined MacDonald and the two

uniformed men at the other end of the twisting passage.

'Found anything?' he rapped.

'No sign of Van Grote or Miss Duncan. I'm waiting a report from my men combing the upper floors. Incidentally, there are still two rooms below this cellar level, Inspector. Like to look?' He showed Ian the narrow, steep flight of steps that led down to two square cellars furnished as rooms. Ian noted the table, chairs and carpets in both rooms.

'How the devil there is any ventilation down here is a mystery,' he growled. He paused. 'Doesn't seem to be anybody here.'

MacDonald agreed.

'Always the same. What can we do? How can we even prove Van Grote to have been here? And even if we find him, we've got to make a case against him.'

'Shouldn't be difficult with two of his men dead in the grounds of Duncan House,' said Ian dryly.

The other shook his head gloomily.

'Van Grote is clever.' Ian ruffled the carpet with his foot. He bent down and lifted a corner, and heaved the table to one side and quickly rolled back the carpet. He stamped round the bare boards. They seemed to be sound enough.

'Looking for another staircase?' inquired MacDonald. 'Hardly seems likely to be another cellar-level. We are two floors below ground already.'

'Might as well try.' muttered Ian worriedly.

He walked into the other room, flung the table back, and heaved at the carpet.

The floorboards seemed as sound as the other room until Ian's stamping foot caused one portion of the floor to rattle. He bent to examine the joints of the planks. He whipped out a clasp knife and inserted it in the aperture.

'Found something?' inquired Mac-Donald with interest.

'A trapdoor,' said Ian briefly.

He hauled the door suddenly back on its hinges, and they peered down at a rectangle of solid shadow.

'We need a light,' said MacDonald, and he took a large electric torch from his pocket. He shone it down a flight of stairs.

'I'm going down,' said Ian.

'Well, I'll join you.'

And so they came to the passage, which held the three rooms hired by Van Grote. But when Ian, MacDonald and the two constables examined the underground suite, there was no one to be seen. They ran into yet another passage that was evidently a dead-end. The doors from the three rooms led on to it, but it was a blind alley. At the far end of the passage, away from the cul-de-sac, they found another cellar.

But it was empty.

★　★　★

Van Grote and his men plunged noisily along the deserted sewer, taking Shirley with them. The Gunner volunteered to stand by a corner in the tunnel, his gun ready.

At the sound of the first shot the others would know that the police had found the secret door and were after them.

Yards above him, Ian was showing MacDonald the cigarette-ends on the floor.

'Someone has used these rooms recently. These cigarette-ends look fresh. If it was Van Grote and his men, how the devil have they got away?'

'I don't see how they could have time to climb through the trapdoor and replace the carpet. Even then they would have to climb another floor — so far as I can see — to get out,' agreed Mac-Donald.

'I can't find any trace of Miss Duncan,' said Ian bitterly.

'If Van Grote and his men have been hiding in these rooms — and I would not be surprised at that — it means there is another exit somewhere.'

They looked round the rooms again. One door of each room led into the passage, which ran to the trapdoor. The other door in each room led to the seemingly blank tunnel. Ian went into the tunnel, and examined the walls and floor with the aid of MacDonald's electric torch, but he failed to find the cunningly designed stone-slab, which pivoted to give access to the last hole. True, he examined every cranny of the passage. But there were a number of similar stone slabs, all apparently solid, and it seemed impossible that there was any exit, secret or otherwise, from this passage.

Full of anger at his rebuff, Ian returned to the room and felt the metal frame of the electric fire. It was still warm to his touch.

'This has not even had time to cool!'

'It's damnable,' said MacDonald. 'But it may be that Van Grote and his men were hiding in some other room.'

'There's no real evidence they were ever here,' said Ian reluctantly.

They climbed back to the level where the crazy passage ran through the building. By this time, it seemed, policemen were everywhere. One or two undesirables had been discovered in the upper storeys, and removed, but there was no sign of the gangsters.

A sudden idea came to Ian Boyd, a risky idea but one that might give results. It was all too plain that a frontal raid on

Ahmed Fey's place would always prove fruitless. Spellwing's testimony seemed sound. The man was telling the truth because he was scared stiff. So apparently Van Grote and the rest of the mob had some secret way of escape in the event of a raid.

But what if one man could enter Ahmed Fey's house unrecognised?

When the police-cars were on their way back to Headquarters, Ian put his idea before MacDonald.

'You tell me that Ahmed Fey holds regular gaming-parties. I'd like to wangle my way into one of these parties — tonight, if he holds one. How did that secret agent you told me about get an invitation?'

'Through an informer. Ahmed Fey issues invitations to potential pigeons after he has satisfied himself they are not from the police. I don't suppose he bothers much about who the mugs are, so long as they appear to have some money. If you would like to get in, we'll contact our man and see what we can do. What do you propose to do?'

'Simply get into the building without raising any alarm as we have just done. I'd have to play cards I suppose, but I might get the chance to snoop around. Remember, I feel keenly about the possibility of Miss Duncan's being imprisoned in a dump like that.'

MacDonald, who was something of a student of human nature, smiled.

'Not a bad idea, though I warn you it is risky. Anyway, if you don't come out by a pre-arranged time we'll stage another raid.'

'Good,' said Ian. 'I hope Ahmed Fey is holding one of his little games tonight. I don't want to waste time.'

MacDonald glanced at the other's broad shoulders and smiled again.

'I can't imagine you doing that,' he said.

11

Double-Death

Van Grote was in a rage. His eyes smouldered and his movements as he walked to-and-fro across the room were slow and ominous. The Gunner, Ted Morris and Nick Murdoch were wisely silent except when a remark was obviously necessary and then Nick spoke up.

'So the cops have got Spellwing, and Bob Holt is dead!' snapped Van Grote. He sneered: 'Pretty easy to see who squealed. Spellwing, white-livered swine! That nosey special got on to Spellwing too damned easily for my liking. Now I've got to get another engineer. Damned good thing I made Spellwing make some tracings! I still have the seven sheets of the drawing.'

They had returned to the three rooms beneath Ahmed's place and Van Grote had vented some of his venom on Ahmed

Fey, but even so he was worried. They had nearly been trapped. Until Morton Sankey got out the alibis, Grote and his men would not dare risk being picked up.

'But the cops won't stop me,' continued Van Grote sombrely. 'I'll get that machine made, and the explosive manufactured. I'll get the remainder of the drawing.'

'You contact this Marcus Williams' guy, boss, and I'll rub him out,' said the Gunner quietly.

Van Grote nodded approval.

'That's the idea! I'm going to risk phoning Sankey. I want him to locate this Marcus Williams guy for me. After that you can get busy, Jack,'

There were two risks for Van Grote. He had to chance leaving his bolt-hole near the secret door and go upstairs to Ahmed Fey's room. And he had to talk very guardedly to Sankey.

Morton Sankey, who was as crooked as a corkscrew, listened and replied in monosyllables.

Satisfied, Van Grote went back to his hideout.

Marcus Williams sat at his hotel table and stared grimly at the carefully placed sheets of paper before him.

Myra Williams was irritated. Success in this exploit always seemed to be just out of reach. If Marcus didn't acknowledge the fact, it was still true that their money was running out. Living in hotels cost money! Unless there was some income shortly, they would have to consider some other highly profitable little exploit as a sideline to this main venture.

'Five sheets,' repeated Marcus Williams. 'I tell you, I'm damned if I know how this happened. I could swear I grabbed the whole drawing from that old fool Ramsay Duncan. But five sheets!'

'Fairly obvious that this isn't the whole drawing!' snapped Myra. 'They'd hardly be numbered 8 to 12!'

'Don't I know it!'

'The rest must be still at Duncan House,' she said.

He stared across the table. They were breakfasting in their room and his tea was growing cold while he examined for the tenth time the sheets of paper he had snatched from Ramsay Duncan.

On an impulse, Myra picked up the morning paper, which had been brought in for them.

She could not miss the headlines that screamed at her:

GANG WARFARE AT DUNCAN HOUSE.

MORE GANG MURDERS.

Swiftly she read the account.

While Williams was drinking his cold tea and staring at the drawings, she said quickly:

'Ramsay Duncan has been murdered by Van Grote. Evidently there was a raid on Duncan House some time after you left with that fool Boyd.'

He took the newspaper from her.

'There is no mention of the drawings here,' he said, scanning the paragraphs. 'Usual stuff about gang-terrorism. But this can only mean one thing — Van Grote must have the first seven sheets of Ramsay Duncan's drawings. Hello! Apparently Shirley Duncan has been kidnapped by Van Grote!'

He laughed mockingly.

'It would seem the girl was snatched while our friend Inspector Boyd was hanging desperately to the luggage grid of my car. How ironical!'

Myra leaned forward and read a portion of the column again.

'It doesn't actually mention Van Grote's name in the paper,' she said slowly. 'But there's no doubt who staged the raid.'

'Well, it wasn't us — so he's the only one in the field!' said her husband. 'It's damned bad luck I didn't get all those papers. I was on the spot before him — and if I'd got the complete set of drawings, we should be heading for London now. As it is, I must make another attempt to get the other sheets.'

'And how do you propose to do that?'

He was staring thoughtfully at the newspaper, but he was no longer reading.

'If Van Grote kidnapped Shirley Duncan, he'll make her talk when he sees that only half the drawings are available. He'll ask her for the where-abouts of the other sheets, assuming he guesses that the drawing is incomplete, and I think Spellwing would soon advise him. As I say, he'll make the girl talk, and she knows that I grabbed some of the sheets of paper! Therefore, by now, Van Grote is aware that I have the last five drawings, in the set.'

'He'll be after you,' said Myra swiftly.

Marcus Williams smiled easily.

'But I am expecting him, or some of his underlings, so I am forewarned.'

'Why not sell your part of the drawing to Van Grote?'

'My dear, the complete drawing is worth thousands to us. It is unlikely that Grote would pay up to that price.'

'It would be the easiest way out.'

'That is not what I'm looking for.'

'I tell you Van Grote is dangerous,' she snapped, her irritation welling up again.

'Don't lose your temper,' he said suavely. 'I know what danger I'm facing. Now let me see. If Van Grote contacts me, it will save me the trouble of finding him. If he is hiding, and I suspect he is, I will learn where to strike. Lone-wolf tactics, my dear. Van Grote with his bold methods is either a fool or a clever man. Probably a mixture of both. I have often found that in outstanding men.'

She rose from the table and left him. She went to the bedroom, and with a hard laugh looked into the mirror and began to brush her hair.

Marcus Williams leisurely read the remainder of the newspaper and finished his breakfast. His mind revolved many schemes, but they all depended on Van Grote making the first move.

It was about an hour later, when he and Myra were sitting in the hotel lounge in company with others before a cheerful fire, that Morton Sankey was shown in to them.

Morton Sankey was plump and suave. He could think in six ways at once, and each one was crooked! Outwardly, he appeared to be a successful elderly professional man. That he was a disgrace to an honest profession a few suspected but could not prove. He held out a pink hand to Marcus Williams.

'Mr. Williams, I believe,' he said softly. He always spoke softly, but at the moment he was anxious that the other occupants of the lounge should not hear the exchange of conversation.

Marcus Williams inclined his head and smiled.

'My name is Morton Sankey, and I am a lawyer, Mr. Williams. I — er — should like to talk to you on behalf of — ah — a friend.'

Marcus Williams smiled again and introduced Myra.

'Should we go to our rooms?' he suggested.

'Excellent idea.'

They ascended by the lift, and Marcus Williams gave an order for coffee to be sent up. Over the steaming cups, Morton Sankey began to explain.

'I have found you only after considerable exertion. At least, I have had several messengers out making inquiries at the hotels. From my information I was told you would be living at an hotel — probably a well-known one. Do you know how many hotels there are in this town? My messengers were certainly fortunate enough to find you quickly.'

'And you have contacted me on behalf of Van Grote, suggested Marcus Williams sardonically.

'Yes,' said Morton Sankey unemotionally. 'He would like to arrange a little business deal with you.'

'Why doesn't he come in person?'

The lawyer permitted himself a smile.

'Van Grote leads an odd existence. At the moment he is in difficulties — temporary, of course.'

'Well, what does he suggest?' demanded Marcus Williams.

'He has told me to say he will pay you five hundred pounds for some papers you possess.'

Morton Sankey fixed bright eyes expectantly on the other.

Marcus Williams laughed contemptuously.

'Five hundred!' he repeated incredulously. 'Does our big shot call that money?'

'Candidly, I do not know the nature of these papers Van Grote desires,' explained

Morton Sankey patiently. 'So I cannot pass judgment upon the price offered. However I am not empowered to offer any more. Van Grote was emphatic. The price is five hundred pounds. What is your answer?'

'The answer is: nothing doing!' said Marcus Williams coarsely.

Morton Sankey rose.

'Thank you for the coffee, Mr. Williams. I shall give Van Grote your answer.' He looked at the gold wristwatch on his pink wrist. 'Well, I cannot allot any more time to Van Grote's affairs.' He glanced sharply at Marcus Williams. 'You know, of course, that Van Grote is a very — er — hasty man?'

'So am I!' snapped the other.

Secretly, he was wondering if Morton Sankey's visit held some other significance.

At this Morton Sankey seemed to lose all further interest. Within a minute he was outside the hotel, hailing a taxi.

'Well, you turned down the five hundred,' commented Myra, and she glanced at the brooding face of the man beside her. He turned to her. They were sitting on the settee.

'You know that would hardly cover expenses so far. I wonder if that was a genuine offer?'

'Of course it was genuine. Van Grote could do big things with that complete drawing.'

'Yes, I know it was genuine in so far that Van Grote would willingly have paid five hundred for the drawings I have, but I can't help thinking he knew I would turn the offer down. You see, he doesn't intend to pay any more. Yet he has located me now. This requires some thinking out.'

Myra Williams rolled back her dress and tugged the tiny little automatic from the elastic straps that held it to her thigh.

'If he starts anything, I'll get in some shooting practice,' she said grimly.

But the usual easy smile that adorned Williams's face had gone. He sat thinking, brooding in a sombre manner.

Suddenly he said: 'Van Grote will send a man to get the drawings. We've got to beat that man and make him talk. I want to find out where Van Grote is hiding out.'

*   *   *

It was an hour later that the Gunner came to the hotel where Marcus Williams and Myra were staying. He came armed with two automatics and the description of Marcus Williams, which Van Grote had obtained from Morton Sankey.

The Gunner was looking his most inoffensive as he talked to the clerk at the reception desk.

'I should like to see Mr. Marcus Williams on a matter of business. He is expecting me.'

If his potential victims were out, other plans would have to be made on the spur of the moment. The Gunner's plans were in the main very simple; he intended to kill Marcus Williams and obtain the drawings, and if the woman got in the way, he would kill her, too.

A page showed Jack the Gunner up to a room on the second floor. Halfway along the passage, the gangster paused and said:

'Here you are, boy. I can announce myself to Mr. Williams.'

He handed two silver coins to the surprised youth, and waited until he had disappeared down the stairs. Then he walked slowly to the door of the Williams's room.

He tried the door, and found it open. He sidled through.

His gun was ready, with safety catch off. He saw the figure lying on the settee. It was a man and he was asleep.

'All right, mug. Get up slowly.'

He waited for another second and then crossed with lithe steps to the settee. He poked the figure in the back with his upraised foot.

The next instant a gun exploded and Jack the Gunner's automatic jumped from his hand.

Even as he nursed his numb fingers, a man emerged from the bedroom door. It was Marcus Williams, the man he had come to kill. In Williams's hand was an ugly gun pointed steadily at the gangster.

'Put your hands up,' said Williams.

The Gunner slowly raised his hands.

He had been tricked, decisively tricked. It was the first time in his life and the experience rankled. The figure on the settee was simply a stuffed jacket and a wig. A dressing gown had covered the figure in a manner sufficient to suggest that here was a man having a sleep. Jack the Gunner had known it was a trick the moment his foot touched the decoy but it had been too late. Marcus Williams had timed it nicely.

'You are Van Grote's man,' said Marcus Williams. 'Now where is Van Grote hiding? Not at his own flat after last night's do, I should imagine.'

The Gunner was not wasting time in talk. He did not even listen. His brain was darting swiftly over the possible courses of action left to him. He had another loaded gun in his pocket, and it was a type from which the safety catch had been removed. The Gunner was willing to gamble his life that there were few men quicker than himself on the draw but with his hands above his head it would be impossible to beat the other's advantage. He would be dead before his hands touched his pocket. He was certain that Williams would have no compunction in shooting.

'In a few minutes someone is coming to this room to inquire about that shot of mine,' said Marcus Williams.

'If you don't tell me Van Grote's whereabouts there will be another shot, and you will be dead. You are a notorious gunman. I shall obviously have fired in self-defence. That will be the story. Are you going to speak? I shall count three.'

Marcus Williams paused and then said: 'One.'

'Listen, Mister,' said the Gunner thickly. 'Van Grote is hiding.'

'Where?' asked Marcus Williams, and he added: 'Two!'

'Ahmed Fey's house.'

'I see you *are* talking,' sneered Williams. 'Where is this house?'

'By the river. It's easily found — everybody knows Ahmed.'

'What is the precise nature of the hideout?' asked Marcus Williams.

'It is a cellar.'

'Thanks, but I require fuller details. I

can hardly imagine Van Grote simply sitting in a cellar awaiting the arrival of the police or anyone else through the front door. What sort of cellar is it? Remember, I have counted two.'

'It is a cellar with a secret door,' said Jack the Gunner. 'There are three rooms, and they branch into a tunnel which has a secret door and behind this door there is a getaway. But to get to the three rooms you gotta find the trapdoor.'

'Appears to be a trifle complicated,' commented Marcus Williams, and he frowned.

The Gunner knew it was complicated. He wanted the other to think it was very complicated.

'I could draw you a plan,' said the Gunner quietly.

The other seemed to be considering. Finally he called, 'Myra, come and frisk this fellow. He has offered to draw us a plan of Van Grote's hideout.'

The Gunner cursed inwardly, though his face betrayed not a sign of his discomfiture. At that moment there was an urgent knock on the door outside, and the sound of voices.

'Keep him covered, Myra,' said Marcus Williams. 'That is the management making a row outside.'

He went to the door and opened it slightly.

Myra heard him say, 'I'm so sorry for the disturbance, gentlemen. I was simply cleaning my revolver, and — er — I'm afraid it accidentally exploded. Look, here it is!'

A few more sentences and Marcus Williams closed the door.

'The gullibility of some people has always amazed me,' he commented. 'However, frisk this gentleman, Myra.'

She approached and made the fatal mistake. She passed close to the Gunner, intending to search his pockets from behind him. This was perfectly sound tactics, but the Gunner moved like a cat.

He jumped at her and caught her to him. He was a slender man, but his arms encircled her body with a grip of desperation. She clawed at his face with both hands. At the first impact the gun had flown from her hand. She tried to push him away. She hammered at his head, drawing bloody marks down his face. Jack the Gunner rammed his free hand into his pocket.

Marcus Williams looked for a chance to shoot. If he shot at the encircling arm of the gangster, he could kill Myra. For a second he wavered. Should he shoot? There seemed not one inch of the man, except his arm, at which he could aim.

And then Jack the Gunner pressed the trigger of the gun in his pocket. The bullet seared the cloth before boring a neat hole in Marcus Williams's head. Myra shrieked.

Williams's mouth jerked open his eyes widened, suddenly he slid to the ground, his gun a futile weapon now that the hand which grasped it had lost all feeling.

Jack the Gunner thrust the woman savagely from him and as she staggered back screaming, he pumped two shots into her. Myra's screams ended abruptly, and she collapsed like a rag doll.

The killer wasted not a fraction of a second. Earlier his careful eye had spotted the exact position of the fire escape. That must be his exit, but first he must try to discover the drawings.

Marcus Williams was the obvious choice. Jack the Gunner heaved him over, and thrust a hand through his pockets with quick, hasty movements.

He found the folded sheets of paper immediately in the inside jacket pocket. A second later he darted for the window. He rammed it open and climbed out with swift movements. His feet began to clatter as he ran quickly down the iron stairs towards the hotel courtyard below.

12

The Last Round

The murders at the hotel in Jamaica Street hit the afternoon editions of the evening newspapers, but long before the public read of the latest murders, Detective-Inspector Boyd hurried along to identify the dead man and woman. With the usual crowd of police specialists, photographers and fingerprint men, came Detective-Inspector MacDonald.

'This is the end of Marcus and Myra,' said Ian to MacDonald. 'This is a typical gangster murder. A double killing in cold blood, carried out by a desperado. God! It's inhuman.'

'This is the type of crime we are up against,' commented MacDonald grimly. 'The gunman got clean away in the usual confusion. Obviously one of Van Grote's thugs, if he came after the Duncan drawings.'

'Marcus Williams had half the pages,' said Ian. 'But now it seems that Van Grote has achieved his object, and has the full set of drawings.'

'And has committed wholesale murder to get them.'

Later, back at Police Headquarters, Ian Boyd and MacDonald sat at a table and discussed their plans. With them was a representative of the flying squad and a detective-sergeant.

'It is certain Van Grote is hiding in Ahmed Fey's warren,' concluded Mac-Donald. 'I've got extra men all round the district. If we can't find him at the moment, it is certain he can't move out without being seen, night or day. We've got to get him before some clever fellow manufactures evidence to prove that Van Grote was nowhere near Duncan House. Oh, it has been done previously. A whole series of men and women bob up with stories proving that Van Grote or some of his mob, have been at a party or elsewhere. But we'll get him this time. Van Grote has overstepped the mark.'

Ian Boyd had been sent from Scotland

Yard to provide Ramsay Duncan with advice and to investigate the possibility of danger to his valuable discovery. So far he had failed. So his strong itch to smash Van Grote rose out of his sense of duty, but just as strong was the desire to rescue Shirley Duncan from the gangster's clutches at the earliest opportunity.

Always his mind was on the girl. He could not be sure, but it seemed likely that Van Grote would keep her a permanent hostage in case anything went wrong with his plans. Anyway, within a few hours Ian would do his damned best to set her free.

It was later in the day when Ian's scheme was set a-foot. Dusk had fallen a few hours previously. Ian left the Police Headquarters in a car driven by a plain clothes man, but the car merely took him to a side street some blocks away and set him down.

Few people would have recognised him. True, his great height could not be altered, but everything else about him was. He was dressed in a chalk-striped suit with ornamentations in the way of half-belts, and pleated pockets. Ian's face was rather different from his usual cheerful, lean visage. He had acquired a short moustache, and the flesh round his eyes was puffy. His dark hair was now gingery and had been parted in the middle. Something had been done to his cheeks, and they seemed to match the puffiness of his eyes.

In general, Ian now looked a picture of dissipation. The expert at Police Headquarters had spent two solid hours in altering his appearance, and it had been a painful two hours. The puffy appearance of his eyes was due to an injection under the skin. His cheeks had been extended with ingenious pads, and he had had to learn how to talk with these in position.

Ian left the police car and stepped out to his appointment with the police informer, who had procured two invitations to Ahmed Fey's gaming party that night. Unruffled by the police raid, the man intended to carry on with his profitable parties, if only to indulge an innate love of gambling.

Ian contacted the informer at the

appointed rendezvous. They exchanged greetings and the caution in the informer's voice was noticeable.

'What do you say to a taxi, mate?' said Ian, deciding to talk in character from the start.

'Okay with me,' grunted the other, whose name was Munro. He was a little man who hardly smiled. His face was lined and crafty.

Ian was armed with a gun, a knife, police whistle and a pocket stuffed with pound notes. In the taxi, he said to Munro: 'You got plenty o' cash chum?'

'No. Ah could do wi' ma money in advance,' grunted the man.

Ian paid him.

They were admitted to Ahmed Fey's house after being scrutinised in a lighted passage. Munro tendered his grubby cards to the Arab, while Ian essayed a jaunty grin. He stuck his hands in his trouser pockets and slouched. His red tie dangled ridiculously. Ahmed glanced at the two men with impassive face.

'This is my pal, Tim Harper,' said Munro.

Ahmed Fey inclined his head. He still seemed to hesitate.

'There is little playing tonight,' he began. Ian grinned and showed the Arab a wad of notes. They were mostly grimy notes, but there were at least one hundred and fifty of them.

'I got three other wads, mate,' he hinted. 'I'm looking for a good game.'

'Come off it, Ahmed,' said Munro, unsmilingly. 'I got some dough. The last time I was here you lifted two hundred quid out o' ma pocket.'

Ahmed Fey's role was invariably that of host playing with his guests. Those who suspected crooked play often cut up rough, but the Arab had hired thugs who acted as his bodyguards. Ahmed allowed others occasionally to win; it gave his gambling parties an air of honest dealing. At all events, he was usually more than well repaid.

Munro and his companion were taken along the rambling ground floor passage towards Ahmed Fey's room. Ian Boyd slouched along, hands in pockets, grinning like a fool. When they entered

Ahmed's living room, the man led them towards a seemingly blank wall.

'Say, mate, you on the square?' demanded Ian and he leered at Munro

'It's all right, mon,' retorted Munro. 'I tell you I been here before.'

Suddenly, Ian and Munro found themselves looking at a door in a wall, which had previously seemed solid.

Ian wondered if this was the entrance to the rooms, which hid Van Grote and Shirley. His heart beat quicker, but he still maintained his careless attitude.

They passed through the door and it closed silently behind them. For the moment they were in darkness, and then Ahmed opened another door and they passed into a brightly lit room. The air was warm and smoke-filled. There were several tables, but at the moment only two were in use.

Four men sat at one table and they hardly raised their eyes from their cards as Ian entered with Ahmed and Munro. The men were of various types. One was a bald-headed individual who looked like an ex-pugilist. Actually he had retired from the ring many years ago and now was the fortunate owner of a billiards-hall. However, he preferred poker to billiards. Two of the other men were typical 'racing' men. They were spare-built and leather-faced. The fourth man was a Chinaman, with nothing about him to suggest he was the first mate of a Chinese tramp steamer lying in the river.

Ian's heart thudded when he saw Ted Morris sitting at the other table in company with a thin, undersized man. Although Ian did not realize it, he had been a famous jockey until expelled from the turf for 'throwing' a race. Still, he seemed to have money. He was placing pound notes against Gentleman Ted's on a simple gamble known as 'cutting the cards'.

Ted Morris flicked his eyes over Ian and Munro and then he looked inquiringly at Ahmed Fey.

'More players, Ahmed?' he drawled.

Ahmed gave the names — Harper and Munro. Ian leered and placed his wad on the table.

'What about a game o' poker?' he demanded.

'Not a bad idea,' said Gentleman Ted. 'I'm sick of losing money to my friend here.'

The jockey showed his yellow teeth in a grin and his eyes swept over Ian and Munro calculatingly. Ahmed Fey drew up a chair and brought out a new pack of cards, breaking the seal before their eyes.

As gamblers they were there for only one reason, to enjoy the risk and excitement of winning or losing. But their main intention was to win, and they watched one another as if they were enemies.

Within a few minutes the game was moving swiftly, the players silent, tense, only their brains working unceasingly as they watched the run of the cards. Little was spoken for fully half an hour, the only movement being the flick of cards, the rustle of notes and an occasional comment. Ted Morris and the jockey smoked in chain fashion, and Ian kept a cigarette dangling limply from his lip. Munro played earnestly, intending to win as much as possible before the dick by his side decided there were other ideas besides gambling all night. Ian lost some money and glared at the others. He had to act a part — that was the better half of his disguise. He enjoyed the knowledge that Ted Morris had not recognised him.

After an hour's play, Morris had won a considerable amount. The jockey was sullen, while Ian, who had done most of the losing, glared convincingly. Ahmed Fey was impassive.

Ted Morris threw away his cigarette in disgust.

'This damned thing has me parched. Gosh, I could do with a drink.'

'Same here, mate,' growled Ian.

'I've got a bottle of whisky in my room,' said Ted. 'Care to have one with me?'

'Anything you like,' bragged Ian, and he got up. 'Excuse us, gents. Break for liquor!'

Quietly, he exulted in the thought that this was the chance he had been awaiting.

Ahmed Fey passed a warning glance to Ted Morris as they moved towards the door of the room. Ian noticed the expression and guessed the man did not want Ted Morris to be careless in showing the stranger around.

Ted Morris led the way through Ahmed Fey's room, he seemed to know the secret of the hidden door — and they walked together down the passage.

Morris took him to the two rooms of which one had the trapdoor under the carpet. As Morris stooped to heave up the trapdoor, Ian struck him one accurate blow on the back of the head with his gun-butt. Ted subsided on the boards. without so much as a groan. Ian worked quickly. In the other room was a cupboard large enough to accommodate the 'con' man, which locked from the outside. Ian guessed that Ted Morris would be out for a long time after such a blow.

With Morris out of the way, he cautiously raised the trapdoor and descended the stairs into a dimly lighted passageway. The very fact that Ted Morris had intended to show him down here was proof that the gangsters had their hideout nearby. He would have to act quickly. It was now or never! If he stayed away too long from the gaming-room, Ahmed Fey would become suspicious.

In the light of a solitary yellow electric light bulb, he crept along the passage and stopped to listen outside the three doors.

Behind one there was definitely the sound of voices. He heard a dead monotone, as if someone was discussing a subject at great length. Ian wondered how many men were in the room. He wondered if it was Van Grote and his gangsters. He bent down to a keyhole.

It was a few seconds before he actually saw the squat figure of the gang leader move into the limited oval of vision, which the keyhole afforded. The glimpse was momentary, but Ian knew it was his man. At Police Headquarters, Ian had been furnished with a complete and careful description of the gangster.

He tried the door handle, listening to the droning voice intently. If it faltered or stopped in any significant fashion, it might mean that the slowly turning handle had been noticed. Ian perspired as he gripped the doorknob and turned. He paused a second to eject the uncomfortable pads from his cheeks. He had no need for them now. The balloon was going up!

He ascertained that the door was not locked, and braced himself. He crashed into the room a second later and received a photographic impression of Van Grote and three other men. In another second Ian was shooting in order to defend himself.

Already he had seen one of the men reach for the bulky gun in his jacket pocket.

Crash! Crash!

The detonations in the confines of the room were terrific. Acrid smoke swirled from Ian's gun. Jack the Gunner was beaten before he tried to draw, chiefly because Ian had the advantage of surprise. The other shot plunged into Nick Murdoch as he attempted to shoot from his jacket pocket The two men sank to the floor with the life sapping from them.

'Don't move you two!' roared Ian to

Van Grote and the other man.

He flung a glance at the bodies on the floor. They were dead or dying. They had lived by the gun and had died that way.

'I want Miss Duncan!' rapped Ian. 'Where is she? Tell me instantly — one of you — or I shoot. I don't give a damn if I kill both of you.'

'This is murder,' said Van Grote hoarsely. 'Who the hell are you to butt in here and start shooting? Don't you know you've killed two men?'

'Two rats, who would have killed me. Come off it, Van Grote. I could kill the lot of you and still get away with it. You're a killer, nothing better. I want Shirley — and Ramsay Duncan's drawings.'

Still Van Grote delayed. There was desperation in his eyes. But he was hoping that some of Ahmed Fey's toughs would hear the shot and come running, and Ian knew it. Ian took careful and deliberate aim at Van Grote's companion. The man suddenly showed a yellow streak. He spluttered into speech before he realised what he was saying.

'The girl is in the room at the other end of the passage!'

'Get moving in that direction,' ordered Ian.

The man ran past into the corridor outside. Van Grote moved slowly. Ian pressed the trigger and a bullet exploded under Van Grote's feet. The gang leader moved more quickly.

They came to the cellar door that was Shirley's prison. Ian turned the key in the lock and ushered his two captives inside. Shirley Duncan was sitting on the grimy bed, pale and tense.

'My God! Shirley! Are you all right?'

As she ran impulsively to him, after the first stare of non-recognition, he was afraid she might cross his line of fire. But she reached him safely, and Van Grote was on the wrong side of his police automatic.

'We haven't a second to lose, Shirley, darling. We've got to get out of here before Ahmed Fey starts something.'

'I'll do as you say!' she said breathlessly.

Ian snapped: 'Get into the passage

again, Van Grote. You, stay here!' he barked to the other gangster. In the passage, Ian turned the key on the man and put it in his pocket. He kept his gun in Van Grote's back all the time.

'Now — move!' he commanded, and they went slowly forward.

But Van Grote's brain was working desperately, and, suddenly he saw his chance. They were just approaching another of the innumerable doors, which studded the walls of Ahmed's house, and it was partly ajar revealing an interior dimly lit by the red glow of an electric stove. As they came level with the door, the gangster whipped quickly round, pivoting on his heel, so as temporarily to thrust aside Ian's gun, and then leaped quickly aside through the half-open door, which he closed after him.

Ian raised his gun and fired point-blank at the panels. He heard a sudden shriek of agony, and raising his foot, kicked open the door.

Van Grote was at the far side of the room, his free hand on the handle of a door that undoubtedly led to the escape tunnel. His face was ashen with pain, and in a flash Ian saw that one of his bullets had struck the desperado in the shoulder, where a spreading red stain coloured the man's jacket. Automatically, Van Grote tugged again at the door, but it was locked! Baffled, he sank to his knees, cursing aloud, and as he did so a small cast-metal box tumbled from his pocket.

'The thuramite!' said Ian, and stepped forward. But with a crazy laugh, Van Grote snatched up the electric-fire and heaved it towards Ian in a last gesture of desperation, the long flex snaking out after it. It fell on the floor almost at Ian's feet, and the sudden, pungent smell of scorching fabric arose as the dirty carpet swiftly caught fire.

Simultaneously, Ian heard feet descending the stairs at the far end of the passageway. He saw Van Grote collapse and jumped across to the other side of the passage, motioning Shirley back against the wall and flattening himself out alongside her, facing down the passage. Suddenly a pale tongue of flame spurted up from the smouldering carpet, then another, and another.

An acrid stench of burning filled the corridor.

Ahmed Fey descended the stairs, and stood watching them — impassive. Ian raised his pistol threateningly and covered the man.

'They say to come quietly,' said Ahmed. 'Without difficulty or my men kill you both.'

Ian said: 'Go to hell!'

Suddenly, Ahmed's head jerked back. He sniffed. Then a look of consternation crossed his face. 'There is burning — burning!' he said.

A pale light, tinged with red, was now shining in the doorway of the subterranean room and Ian looking round, was shocked to see that the flames had taken swift hold of the room — which was lined with match-boarding for walls — and were already starting to lick at the lintel of the door.

'Take this!' commanded Ian, placing the pistol into Shirley's hand. Shielding his face with his arms, he leaped through the curtain of fire; and coughing and spluttering, bent down to raise Van Grote and drag him clear.

He seized the man by the shoulders and partially lifted him — looked closely at him, and straightened up.

Larry Van Grote was dead! The bullet that Ian thought had simply broken his shoulder must have passed into and through his chest. His crimes were at last paid for in full.

A sudden scorching blast of flame seared Boyd's face. The entire room was now blazing around him. He lurched towards the door and out into the passage, coughing and choking.

Ahmed Fey was wringing his hands in mingled fear and desperation. 'My house!' he cried, 'My house!'

'Get upstairs!' snapped Boyd, motioning with his gun. 'And tell your friends that this entire house is surrounded, that there's no escape for any of them. And if you're a good boy and let me get to the police, I'll maybe send for a fire engine! I'd hate you to lose your private gambling den!'

For a second Ahmed hesitated, then his own natural cupidity decided him. He ran up the stairs nimbly, shouting orders in a foreign tongue, then in English: 'Fire! Fire! My house is burning! All is lost!'

Ian and Shirley followed him swiftly, the former holding his pistol grimly in line with the small of Ahmed Fey's back.

* * *

Long afterwards the townsfolk talked about the great disaster by the river, when many blocks of tenement dwellings had been destroyed by a great explosion subsequent upon a fire breaking out in the house of one Ahmed Fey. Thus did the vast power of Ramsay Duncan's explosive make itself manifest for the first and last time. Ian Boyd always blamed himself for failing to retrieve the tiny box of thuramite when it had fallen so opportunely from the keeping of the dying Van Grote almost at his feet.

But his wife would have none of his self-recriminations. 'Darling,' Shirley would say, 'I'm glad to think that there's nothing left of Ahmed Fey's house but wreckage — and that Marcus Williams' part of daddy's plans perished with Van Grote. Daddy would have wished it that way: *now* his secret has vanished — let us hope — forever!'

And Ian Boyd in his heart of hearts would know that she was right and if he had any suspicion that his superiors might have been better satisfied with Ramsay Duncan's invention in their possession, he would least of all admit it to the girl who now followed with anxiety his career at the 'Yard'.

For like all good wives, Shirley Boyd liked to think of her husband as succeeding in his profession; and not merely as the partner of 'the Duncan girl' whose great wealth and possessions made her truly one of fortune's chosen children.

THE END

We do hope that you have enjoyed reading this large print book.

Did you know that all of our titles are available for purchase?

We publish a wide range of high quality large print books including:
Romances, Mysteries, Classics
General Fiction
Non Fiction and Westerns

Special interest titles available in large print are:
The Little Oxford Dictionary
Music Book, Song Book
Hymn Book, Service Book

Also available from us courtesy of Oxford University Press:
Young Readers' Dictionary
(large print edition)
Young Readers' Thesaurus
(large print edition)

For further information or a free brochure, please contact us at:
Ulverscroft Large Print Books Ltd.,
The Green, Bradgate Road, Anstey,
Leicester, LE7 7FU, England.
Tel: (00 44) **0116 236 4325**
Fax: (00 44) **0116 234 0205**

Other titles in the
Linford Mystery Library:

THE RETURN OF MR. BUDD

Gerald Verner

Near Avernley in Berkshire, Superintendent Budd of Scotland Yard is relaxing on holiday at the cottage of his friend, Jacob Mutch. However, Mr. Budd becomes involved in an investigation. He learns from Jacob's neighbour that his cottage has been burgled — twice. Yet nothing was taken. Then the man is found in his cottage brutally murdered. And the following day, the body of a known criminal is found dead nearby, shot through the head!

FOREIGN ASSIGNMENT

Sydney J. Bounds

In the unstable Congo region of Africa, the state of Katanga is an oasis of calm. President Tshombe and his government are united; the country's mines and industries supply the West with copper and uranium. But others, who stand to benefit if the government go under, have plans to assassinate the President. Meanwhile, Detective Simon Brand must prevent the assassination and root out the men behind the plot — and he has just seventy-two hours in which to do it . . .

MOTIVE FOR MURDER

John Russell Fearn

Inspector Mallison was reluctant to arrest the murdered man's son, although the incriminating evidence was overwhelming: he'd been alone with his father immediately prior to the murder and there'd been a bitter quarrel; Goldstein was killed trying to alter his will — unfavourably for his son; the weapon, a desk paperweight bore the son's fingerprints, and his father had withdrawn financial support for a new West End play in which his son was to star. Yet still Mallinson wasn't convinced . . .

RETRIBUTION

Norman Lazenby

Mary Calvin sits in her flat for hours, full of fury and sick with despair for the dreadful waste of her friend's young life, Evelyn Torrance. A dreadful resolution begins to dominate her mind: retribution! Fred Tanner must pay for his crime! She takes sleeping tablets from the medicine chest and selecting a sharp ornamental dagger from the mantelshelf, she slips them into her handbag. She puts on her coat, hurries out and heads for Tanner's flat . . .

LEAVE OVER

Geraldine Ryan

Maternity leave over, DI Casey Clunes is straight back in the thick of it on her return to Brockhaven CID — an unidentified body washed up at Keeper's Cove, a possible arson attack at a nearby amusement arcade and an assault and robbery at a local convenience store . . . And in *A Tough Workout*, joining the local gym benefits Casey's crime-solving along with her fitness levels, as she gets the inside track on a string of local burglaries.